A Case for Line Larsen - Book Two: Heidi Hansen

Lisa J Rivers

FIRST EDITION

Published in 2023 by
GREEN CAT BOOKS
19 St Christopher's Way
Pride Park
Derby
DE24 8JY

www.green-cat.shop

CONTENTS

Heidi Hansen

ACKNOWLEDGEMENTS

"For most of my life, I have had a love of music, in particular, the work of Norwegian 'pop' music band, A-ha.
A-ha have influenced me throughout my life, for almost 40 years, and as an homage to them, all of the chapters in the Line Larsen books are named after the band's song titles."

Chapter 1 – To Let You Win

"Are you moving home, Line?" Aggie enquired, when she saw my bundle of estate agent leaflets.

"Apparently it's necessary," I replied glumly. "My little flat just isn't big enough for the three of us," I explained. "I'm just not sure how we can afford it, seeing as I'm the only one with a job!"

I huffed with dismay, threw Aggie a half-smile and headed for the lift to the office. It took just a few seconds to arrive on the correct floor, which was good as it was way too warm in the confined space. I almost stumbled through the office door, and dumped all my stuff onto my desk. Sitting in my chair, I performed the usual first activities of my day; my bag, containing all valuables and notebooks, placed in my drawer and locked, switched the computer on, then returned downstairs to fetch the coffee jug. It was already filled with water, thanks to Aggie. I reminded myself to thank her later. I shuffled back to the lift and within a minute I was at the coffee machine, filling it with Hansen's favourite coffee.

Yes, Hansen was back – in fact lots of things had changed since Jessica had started her new life; I too had started a new life, but I couldn't help but wonder if she had received a better deal than me. Prison felt… cosy compared to the living arrangements at home; and although she obviously only had one room, at least it was *her* space. Sure, I had a couple more rooms than her, but there was no space of my own anymore.

I absentmindedly switched the coffee machine on and returned to my desk, hoping to have some work to do. I had changed recently though; previously I used to prefer to *earn* my wages, whereas now I was more like Hansen, shudder the thought, and didn't care. I couldn't afford to care.

I now had a little side-job, unpaid of course, discreetly following Hansen, my boss around for his wife, Heidi, who was sure her husband was cheating on her. I was fairly sure myself, as I had spotted him with several different ladies over the last few months. I needed to improve my discretion skills though, as I had been almost caught a couple of times.

Larsen!" he had shouted out loud one day, in Marit's coffee shop, which was packed full of people. "Are you following me?"

"No," I had replied, quickly pressing the icon on my phone, which turned from the camera aimed at him, to instead face me, like I was having an online chat. "Bye," I had exclaimed at this imaginary caller, and shut my phone screen off.

He had continued to stand by my table, and I could see his eyes searching around my table. The blonde still in my peripheral vision was who I had seen him with on a few more successful stakeouts recently. She was fidgeting with boredom, reapplying her makeup repeatedly. She loved herself more than anyone else, that much had been obvious – again backed up during the observations.

He had then spun around on his heel, thrown a glance over to said blonde, sighed and left the shop. The woman stood up, looked out the window and then sat back down again, confused.

"Larsen!" he shouted at me now, too. I blinked myself back to reality. "File these," he barked, throwing some folders labelled 'CONFIDENTIAL' onto my desk.

Since Jessica's case, he trusted me less, once he had found out some of my little investigations. Worse still was that he had terminated Thor's 'working arrangement' when it was unearthed that he had assisted me in my research; well, some of the truth, anyway! I'd felt that he had been lucky to get out, as I desperately wanted to find an alternative to this increasingly depressing situation myself. In fact, I had a bundle of newspapers at home, along with job leaflets for recruitment agencies. I was so unhappy that I wanted to change career totally.

"Become a hairdresser," Astrid had suggested at one of our weekly meetings. "Sure, you'd have to sweep the floor and make hot drinks for the first few months, but we could be together if you worked at my place." I could feel her excitement bubbling as her beautiful blonde curls bobbed around on top of her head. "I'll ask them!" she concluded, downing a whole glass of wine.

We still had our weekly meetings, which now consisted of self-defence classes, before our food treat every Friday night. He wasn't taking that from me. It was the only time I had any fun! Life with Thor, my boyfriend of about six months, had been intense from the moment we finally began our relationship last Christmas. It certainly wasn't what I expected of a relationship, to be honest. My parent's relationship was, tepid I guess, more platonic after all of their years together. On the other end of the scale was Helene, my friend, and her boyfriend, Petter. Both were around the same age as me, but blissfully happy. They both had their own hobbies and interests, as well as joint ones, which seemed to create a perfect combination. Then there was me and Thor, going at a rapid, uncontrollable speed. He had moved in with me after just a few weeks, with his awful brother, Kristian, following a month or two later. We were now cramped in my tiny, one-bedroomed flat.

Glancing at the list of properties I had brought to the office with me, I could see that there was nothing within my price range close to the centre. Thor had made no effort to find a job since Hansen fired him, saying it was because of me that he was now unemployed. Kris had moved in after his parents kicked him out. They had decided to embrace their retirement by selling their home and living on the money in a small log cabin somewhere up north.

Kris had got in the way of their plans, as he too was unemployed. So now I had two houseguests. Why houseguests, I hear you ask – well, because neither make any effort to keep the flat clean and tidy. Sure, I've never been the tidiest of people, but when there is three times the amount of mess there, someone needs to pick up the excess. Working 40 hours a week, followed by cooking when I got home, I felt like I should get a free pass on the housekeeping. Apparently, the boys' online gaming seemed to give them the same free pass too!

I could feel my anger rising, so I ventured into Hansen's office for his daily pastry order. It would do me good to get out into the open. The atmosphere in his office was so thick, you could 'cut it with a knife' as my gran used to say. He glanced up at me, and pulled out his petty cash box. I stood patiently as he counted all the loose change. Despite me never short-changing him, his lack of trust seemed to extend this far, and he had even spent hours checking all of the receipts to see how much he spent. He handed me a wad of loose change and told me to get 'the usual', shooing me out of his office as his mobile phone bleeped.

"Shut the door!" he bellowed.

Down in the lobby, I felt a welcomed breeze. The office and then the lift had been stifling with the summer heat. Aggie had chosen to open up the back door of the building, knowing that it was secure enough that trespassers wouldn't enter. Only a couple of people, those who had worked in this building, knew this entrance even existed. I still didn't like it though. Aggie had been attacked just a few months before, I didn't want her to get hurt again.

She beamed a welcoming smile at me as I approached her desk. "You look a little flustered, Line," Aggie remarked.

"I've never liked the heat," I replied sullenly, "especially trapped in that stuffy office."

"Hansen still not opening the windows, then?"

I shook my head. Hansen had decided that there were too many important documents lying around the main office for the windows to be opened, so only had his own open, as a kind of punishment.

"I'm just so miserable in there," I blurted, tears welling up in my eyes.

Aggie's smile disappeared and a look of concern replaced it. "Come and sit down a few minutes," she suggested.

"I have to get the pastries..."

"A few minutes won't hurt!"

She sat down next to me, a box of tissues in her hand.

I poured my heart out to her; the job, the home life and she just nodded sympathetically.

"Are you still doing that 'side job' for Hormonal Heidi?" she chuckled.

"Yes," I nodded, laughing and blowing my nose simultaneously.

"Might be time to knock that on the head, Line, you don't want to spread yourself too thin. That puny little man needs to man up and look after his wife in the same way that he does with him ditsy mis..."

"LARSEN!" Hansen interrupted her.

My eyes widened as I looked at Aggie. She gingerly stood up and returned to her desk.

"Glad I caught you. Add a hot chocolate to the order, I have a client coming in." I breathed a silent sigh of relief, as he piled more small change into my hand. "And don't forget the receipt!"

"Have I ever forgotten your receipt?" I muttered under my breath, as I ventured into the late morning sun and towards the coffee shop.

The queue at Marit's was long, not surprising since she had introduced fruit slushies and smoothies to her already-delicious menu. My mind worked overtime while I was waiting. How much had Hansen heard? I didn't mind if he heard anything I had said, and although he wasn't Aggie's boss, I didn't want her job threatened in some way.

"Hi, Line," a voice broke my thoughts.

I spun round; it was Kristian.

"Kris... what are you doing here?" I enquired.

"Off to football, but want to grab one of these new slushies. Think I'll go for the ... blue one."

'I just don't care', my mind replied. What I did care about though, was where he had got the money from. I confronted him.

"Ohh, I found it on your bedside table in that little pot. Finders keepers – losers WEEPERS!!"

He hopped in the position in front of me and loudly told Marit what he wanted.

"I really can't stand that... that child!" I told Marit apologetically, as he left the coffee shop.

She smiled sympathetically. "Your usual, Line?" she enquired.

I nodded. "Oh, and a hot chocolate too please," I added.

"Oooh, it's been a while since you had one of those," she chirped.

"Oh, it's not for me, it's for a 'client', apparently."

Marit bagged up all the pastries, with my secret one wrapped separately and handed me the hot drink.

"Bit warm for this, but I'm not judging," I thanked her, rolling my eyes.

"Delightful at any time of the year," she replied.

I placed the goods on the counter and pulled all of the loose change out of my pockets and apologised.

I could feel Marit's mood drop as she stared at it.

"I'm so sorry," I whispered again, shifting uncomfortably.

I could hear those in the queue behind me sigh and tut and I lowered my head.

"You know I trust you, Line, but I just need to count it still," she explained.

I nodded.

I could hear her counting under her breath, then she handed me the receipt.

"Thanks," I muttered, my eyes moistening.

"She upset you, Sis?" Kristian startled me as I left the shop.

I shook my head and hurried back to the office building.

I waited patiently for the lift to arrive. A young lady, no more than 18, with a big chest, tiny waist and more than enough makeup, joined me as we ascended to the correct floor, and shadowed me until we were both in the office.

"Ah!" Hansen burst out of his office, "Hanna, come in, come in," Hansen greeted her enthusiastically. "Larsen, the hot chocolate and pastries?"

I dutifully obliged and approached his office. He stopped me in my tracks.

"Give them here, Larsen," he barked.

I hesitated, as I became aware that my secret pastry was in the same wrapper as his. 'Think, Line, think!'.

I thrust the hot chocolate into his hand and walked over to the coffee machine, placing his pastries on a plate. "Coffee, Mr Hansen?" I offered, smiling politely.

"Ah, yes," he replied.

Perfect! I poured us both a cup and plated up my own pastry.

As I returned to his office and handed him his delights, I observed that the blonde was seated in a chair, her short skirt showing more than I wished to see.

"You are to spend the remainder of the day with Mrs Johnsen." He waved his hand over a pile of folders that he had dumped on my desk. "Take these with you, you can sort them alphabetically while you are there." I briefly examined the workload along with my coffee and snack. "Lock the door on your way out," he concluded.

I retrieved my belongings from the locked drawer of my desk and slipped the pastry back into its wrapper and then into the bag. The folders were more cumbersome than expected, so I abandoned the hot drink and proceeded to Aggie's workspace.

She was as surprised as me, but proceeded to revert to automatic pilot as she set up the phone lines for Hansen to be transferred to her own switchboard. I'd never been behind her desk before, and now found that it was quite complex. Lights blinked on the switchboard machine constantly. How she knew which ones to respond to, I hadn't a clue.

She disappeared into the office behind the reception desk, which I didn't even know existed and returned with a very comfortable chair. "Make yourself cosy, Line," she smiled.

Her very large desk, which curved into a half-moon shape, had 2 main sections; the top part was for visitors to said desk, which she would use to give or receive documents and the like, and the bottom half, which contained all of her work items, such as notebook, computer and of course, the massive switchboard. Beneath the double desk, was another array of shelves strewn with a variety of folders.

I shuffled my new chair to a corner of the desk, away from visitors and from Aggie, to not get in her way, and placed my work on the lower part of the desk, which was waist high. She sat back into her chair and scooted over to the computer, answering a call on the phone as she did so. She grabbed a pen and started making notes as she talked. Once the call was concluded, she popped up from her chair and disappeared into the kitchen. I felt flustered for a few minutes, worried that someone might enter the building, or a phone call would flash on her magic machine, but she returned swiftly, and with two steaming mugs of coffee.

She disappeared again into the back office and returned with a telephone, which she plugged into the wall, behind one of the stacks of folders and then placed on the desk next to me. She tapped into her computer for a couple of minutes.

"There! Now you can answer any calls that come through to your office," she smiled, sipping at her drink.

"How do you keep up with all of this?" I gestured toward her desk.

"Practice – I've been here for a lifetime."

She returned to her duties, and I started mine. I assumed that Hansen wanted the alphabetisation of the surnames of the clients, and realised immediately that the task needed more than originally anticipated, as there were no names on the folders. This would mean that I would need to look at the contents of each one to label and sort them. I hesitated briefly, worried that I might be reprimanded by Hansen, but eventually bit the bullet and opened the first folder. I was greeted with scraps of paper, some stained with coffee cup rings along with spillages of these beverages. I swear I could even smell onion from one of Hansen's greasy burgers on one of the official documents included. I borrowed a pen from Aggie and wrote the name of the first client on the front of the folder. As I returned the documents to their original folder, I noticed that one of the documents referred to the client being a 'she' rather than the 'he' as per the name on the folder. I frowned and took out the remaining documents. Maybe all three were connected to the one case? Should I change the name on the folder, I pondered. Could I legally sort through the documents, when there were confidentiality clauses? Not just with Aggie, but with any visitors to the building possibly gaining access to the documents. I put this one aside for now and moved on to the next: Kari Nordmann #14. Jessica. Jessica Smith, the young girl I tried to save from prison last year. I had thought life was complicated back then, but it was nowhere near as bad as it was now. At least work was keeping me busy enough to not think about my crappy home life.

I wondered how Jessica was doing with her incarceration in Halden. I had hoped to visit her more often, but had only managed a couple of weekend trips on the bus before Thor had moved in. We had made a small start on Jessica learning some Norwegian, and in turn for me to learn a little English, by simply pointing to items and calling out their name. If only she was a free woman, then we would be able to bond more…

"So, show me these lovely houses, Line?" Aggie broke my train of thought. I sighed. "What? Don't focus on the negatives – life's too short for all that. If you *have* to move house, then make sure it is somewhere equally lovely or better, chick."

As I pulled out the papers from my bag, the pastry fell onto the desk, spraying crumbs all over. I panicked and apologised profusely. She leaned over me, scooped up the flaky pieces and swept them into a nearby bin.

"There! Nothing to apologise for!"

"Let's have another cuppa and split this pastry, shall we?" I suggested, standing up and swiping her mug before Aggie had time to protest. I made a mental note to buy one extra to give to my new colleague.

When I returned with the necessary convoy of crockery and cutlery, Mr Olsen, the owner of the building and Aggie's boss had arrived and was talking to Aggie. Should I return to the kitchen? I paused. I didn't want Aggie to get into trouble. I started backtracking to the kitchen when the mugs chinked together, and Mr Olsen turned to look in my direction.

"I see you are settling in well, Miss Larsen," he smiled.

He beckoned for me to join them.

"W…would you like a coffee, Mr Olsen?" I offered.

He shook his head. "No thank you. I'm not stopping too long. I was just checking that you are ok with the new workspace dynamics."

I smiled and looked at Aggie, not 100% sure that I knew what he meant.

"We have created a lovely cubbyhole for her," Aggie laughed.

"Fantastic," he replied.

I matched his smile, and saw the deep lines on his face, possibly through stress and worry, I mused.

He tapped his hand on the desk, his wedding ring echoing around the immediate space. "I shall leave you both. I have a couple of meetings in the city this afternoon. If there are any issues, just let me know, Agnes."

He nodded to me and exited the building.

I breathed an audible sigh of relief and Aggie laughed.

"He won't hurt you," she said.

I placed her mug next to her, and cut the pastry in half, passing her one piece, along with the housing papers, then sat down on my new chair.

"So you need a two-bedroomed home then?" she confirmed. I nodded. "They are quite expensive, though."

"I don't really have a choice, do I?"

Aggie nodded. "Well, yes, you do, unless those two layabouts get a job too!"

I grimaced. "My current flat is very small, yet it costs over half of my wages. My parents had to be my guarantor and had to help with the deposit. Anywhere else, and I'm looking at two to three times more- literally out of my price range!"

She passed the paperwork back to me and ate her pastry half. I slid the house info under my work folders; out of sight, out of mind, and ate mine.

"What are your plans for the weekend?" Aggie broke the silence.

I smiled, my caffeine and sugar levels increased. "Friday night! Woo! It's self-defence followed by dinner with the usual suspects. Then recovering from Friday night on Saturday. Sunday – not sure yet. You?"

"An exciting weekend of gardening!"

"Smashing!" I laughed.

~

The rest of the afternoon flew by, with us both laughing and drinking and eating – rather like how I anticipated my girls' night out later would be.

With just 10 minutes left, Hansen appeared with 'Hanna'. He watched as she left and came to see how I had got on with my work. I had managed the basics of adding a name to a folder as presented to me originally, and sorted them alphabetically. I briefly discussed the confusion regarding the inner documents, but he dismissed my idea and told me to put them all away in the filing cabinets. I did just this, and then by the time I returned to the ground floor,

Hansen had left for the night.

"Seeya then!" I muttered to myself.

"See you on Monday, Line," Aggie said, fetching her belongings and waiting for me to leave. "Let's hope you have a better time with your friends than you do with the wasters you live with," she chuckled, pulling one of her faces. "And don't think about Mr H and his blonde girlfriend!" she laughed as she ran for the bus home, waving.

I stood outside the office building and looked at my phone.

"My husband has a blonde girlfriend?"

The shriek from behind where I stood shocked me to my core. I swung round to encounter Heidi Hansen, Hansen's wife, way closer than I would have liked. 'Think, Line', I thought, desperately searching for a response. Should I explain that I'd been too busy to keep her updated? Should I lie? I've never been good at lying, and I have always considered a liar to be at the very bottom of the morality chain. On the other hand, what can of worms could I potentially open by revealing this new nugget of information? It was, however, the job I had agreed to take on for the poor woman.

"I'm not 100% sure right now, Mrs Hansen. I don't want to give you false information, so decided to wait until I have more evidence." She opened her mouth, and then shut it again. "There was a lady in his office this afternoon," I continued, "for the whole afternoon. Does that mean it's an affair? Not necessarily. I suggest that you be on your guard and see if you can spot any tell-tale signs, any similar behaviour patterns of his, based on previous affairs."

I felt very confident with my response, but withheld the satisfactory smile, for now.

"Tell your friend to watch her mouth in future. You never know who is listening or who could hurt you in this kind of situation!"

"Are you ok, Line?" a gruff voice interrupted our conversation. "If she thinks about threatening you, I am happy to intervene!"

It was Kristian. He had always had an aggressive manner to him, along with the skill of inputting himself into conflict, stoking the fire.

"Shut up, child!" Heidi responded, fighting fire with fire.

Kristian stepped forward, out of the shade of the building that had kept his presence a secret. Thor stepped forward just a few moments later, holding his brother back, whispering words into his ear to calm him.

I found myself apologising to Heidi; to me, she was far more of a threat than the pathetic youth. She had shown her anger to me last year when she beat me in broad daylight, only a stone's throw away from where we were now. I still shuddered to myself every time I walked that way home.

Heidi stood her ground, not intimidated by the child before her. The whole debacle had, however, attracted a crowd of spectators; a mixture of professional businesspeople, and those who were embarking on their evening activities. Stuck in the middle, I could feel my cheeks become redder with embarrassment. Unfortunately, one of the onlookers was Hansen, who had ditched his blonde, it seemed, and was now marching towards us.

"Get in the car," he growled, through his clenched teeth, grabbing his wife by the elbow.

"ARE YOU SLEEPING WITH A BLONDE GIRL?" Mrs Hansen yelled at him defiantly.

"We. Will. Continue. This. At. Home!" he replied, eager to avoid a public slanging match.

Neither party wanted to back down, but the strength of Hansen overpowered his wife's and she was soon bundled into his car, situated just around the corner of the building we had emerged from a few minutes prior. It seemed a lot longer than a few minutes, but now the threat was over, I could relax again.

I turned to look at Thor, just as he sent his younger brother home. He outstretched his hands to console me, to soothe me following what could have been a very explosive situation. I was in his arms in seconds, and he embraced me tightly.

"Come, let's get you home and safe," he whispered tenderly in my ear.

Chapter 2 - Cosy Prison

The next day, I awoke to find a couple of missed calls and a text message from Belle, my best friend. I replied to her text immediately, apologising profusely for my absence last night. I had been shuffled back to my flat after the incident with the Hansens, and tended to by Thor, who plied me with hot chocolate and supper. It seemed that Kristian had been reprimanded by his older brother, as he was nowhere in sight until after we had proceeded to bed. It had been the only evening alone that we had shared since Kristian had moved in, and it had been lovely; just right! I had hoped for him to not return at all, but that clearly wasn't likely.

"What a wretched woman she was!" Kristian announced, as he awoke from the sofa I had just tiptoed past, which he used as his bed. "That... that scorned wife of his." I nodded. "Are you obliged to engage with her?" he continued.

'Good morning, Kristian', I thought to myself. "She was extremely scorned when I first encountered her," I replied, "she even thought I was her husband's mistress."

"WOW!" he grunted. "What happened there then?"

"Well, she confronted me, beat me quite badly..."

"WOW!" he repeated. "So how is she allowed to talk to you?"

"She first attacked Aggie, my work colleague, then came after me. I managed to convince her that instead of beating me more, I should instead investigate her husband's philandering. I have just been keeping my promise."

"Yeah, but once she's away from you, you didn't need to stick to your side of the bargain."

"I put myself in her place. Not with my boss as my partner of course, as I can't stand him. But, how I'd feel if my other half was cheating. Frustrated, upset, betrayed. I'd want answers, so does she."

"Yeah, but she could seriously hurt you."

I pondered this thought for a moment or two. Coffee. That's what I needed right now. I ventured to the kitchen area, tripping over Kris' boots.

"Move your goddamn boots!" I screeched in frustration.

Frustration which had become as part of my daily life, as searching for the coffee pot was. This was the only part of my life that seemed to have any routine right now. I found said coffee pot, shoved at the back of the work surface where it was still plugged in, and switched it on. I found myself wading through a toaster, several used mugs, the butter, a variation of different-sized plates and a carton of opened milk, cap removed. I flapped my hands up and down, not quite knowing where to begin.

The milk was no longer drinkable, that was a given. I tipped the contents down the sink, which was full with more crockery and cutlery. I cursed to myself, trying to find space in the bin to dispose of the empty milk carton. I shoved all of the dirty pots over to the sink, stacking them as carefully as I could, before realising that I needed space in the sink to wash the coffee pot! I rubbed my head in despair, and decided to use the kettle instead, which just needed to be plugged into the socket where the toaster had been. While the kettle boiled, I popped the toaster into the cupboard. I scoured another cupboard for a clean mug, only finding one clean wine glass. That would do, I decided.

I shuffled over to my chair, which had a few of Kristian's clothes on it, and so I threw them onto the sofa.

To avoid any further unnecessary conversations, pre-caffeine, I reached for my earphones, which had been shoved onto the floor next to my chair, and chose some relaxing music to listen to on my phone. I closed my eyes, in an attempt to shut out every possible distraction.

"LEEEEENA!!" the voice broke my brief repose.

I looked up to find Thorfinn staring at me, waving the coffee jug in his hand. I pulled out my earphones to face his confrontation.

"LEEEEENA!" he repeated. "So you made yourself coffee, but were too selfish to make one for all of us?! This one," he continued, waving the pot at me again, "is disgusting. It's from yesterday…"

I cut him off, "Yes, it is from yesterday. Would it hurt you to clean the coffee pot out so that someone can use it the next day?"

"I WAS BUSY BEING YOUR NURSEMAID!" he boomed.

I didn't know how to respond. I was in the wrong, shouldn't have gotten so angry. Tears welled in my eyes, and I apologised, standing up to clean the pots and make a fresh pot of coffee for the whole household. Happy with the harmony returning to the atmosphere, I quickly tidied the sofa and went for a shower.

Once clean and a little happier, I snuggled on the sofa next to Thor, as Kris sat in my chair with his feet on the little coffee table. I wanted to berate him for this, but didn't want to cause more upset.

"Did you get those estate agent's housing lists?" Thor enquired.

"Hmmmnn," I replied sleepily, "in my bag." I sat up to grab my bag from next to the chair, but Kris got there before me and began rummaging through it.

I remained quiet as he passed it to his brother. The properties were listed according to price, from high to low.

"Hmmm," Thor commented, "Ok, we can rule these out," he announced, crossing out all of the flats that had less than two bedrooms. "Ah, here's one," he pressed his long, slender finger on the image of a two-bedroomed flat not far from where *my* flat was. "Two bedrooms, close to the city centre. First floor. Intercom – that'd be great if 'psycho-woman' found out where you lived."

I glanced over at the piece of paper. "That's 35,000 kroner a month!" I exclaimed. "That's more than I earn!"

"We really need to look at you getting a better job, Line. Obviously you are never going to earn a fortune with your lack of qualifications and skills..."

"If three of us are to live somewhere like that, then three of us need to be earning and contributing," I suggested, reasonably.

"I would have a job if your boss hadn't sacked me!"

"You can't get away with taking time off work and spending the boss' money on unnecessary trips."

"Unnecessary trips?" His voice became quite shrill. "We were researching the Kari Nordmann case! It was HIS case!"

"But not with his permission. He was more than happy for her to plead guilty so he could rake in the money straight away. In the end, we ended up getting the result he wanted."

"Exactly my point, Line, it was what he *wanted.*"

"N...no, that's not righ..."

"Did we, or did we not manage to get the guilty plea?"

I didn't have the strength in me to argue anymore. He looked at me with victorious eyes, then returned to the house listings.

"Ok then, if we can't afford that place, let's look for somewhere further out of town."

"I won't be able to get to work if we go further out," I replied, feeling my temper rising again.

"There are other methods of travel than your feet, Line," Kris piped up, clearly thriving on the tension in the home.

"So, public transport will be a new cost to add to the equation, so probably any money we save on renting further away will be swallowed up with travel costs," I tried to explain.

"So, get a bike then!" Kristian replied smarmily, rolling his eyes at me.

"So what you're saying then, Line, is that you don't want to move to a bigger place. That you like living here, all cramped together?"

'What I'm saying, is that maybe your lazy lout of a brother should move out and leave us to get on with life', I thought to myself. I daren't say it out loud, I was sick of the friction as it was.

"What I'm saying is that if we get a bigger place, then the people needing the bigger space should pay their way."

"Like I said, I'd probably have a full-time job by now if Hansen hadn't blacklisted my name!"

"And also like you say, there's other jobs out there than in law. We don't have the luxury of being picky if we want to spend more on rent. And that includes Kris as well, he has to pull his weight and get a job too." I'd felt very courageous at the beginning of that lecture, but felt my voice shying away by the end.

"Right, so we have to go out on a weekend day to look for a job so that you'll be happy?" Thor yelled, as he stood up, throwing the papers along the floor, grabbed his coat and boots and slammed the door.

This action may sound quick, but the angrier he got, the more he fumbled with his laces. Kristian looked on and laughed nervously.

"You needn't laugh, you're not wanted here either, so you better get your shit together and come get a job. On a Saturday. The busiest day of the week, and a day off."

'Day off from what?', I wanted to respond, but I didn't. I was happy for them to both go out, and get a job to boot! Kristian slipped on his boots, opened the front door and stumbled clumsily with untied laces to catch up with his brother.

I sat in silence for a few minutes, waiting to see if they were going to come back. Nothing, not a sound. I smiled outwardly, brushing away a tear of frustration. First things first, I opened the lovely floral curtains of the living room and opened the window for some fresh air. Having men lounging around your home 24/7 produces too much toxic gas! 'In more than one way!'. I then intended to lounge on the sofa and enjoy *my* day off, but could feel the dirty kitchen pots calling me.

Once I'd cleaned the kitchen, I moved onto the bedroom, opening the curtains and window, and stripping the bed. The fresh covers would be a multicoloured floral print, which Thor's masculinity was repelled by. They matched the curtains, with brilliant oranges, yellows, reds and blues almost blooming into the room. I loved these, as they were so cheerful, and I felt uplifted instantly.

I returned to the kitchen, deciding to make dinner. Pasta, the usual. It was cheap and filling, and the boys seemed to enjoy it. Plus, it didn't matter if someone wasn't home, as it could be eaten cold too. I used to make a pasta sauce from scratch, but now I just bought jars, which were just as cheap, but quicker. Once that was popped into the oven, I added some ingredients to my bread maker, which my parents had bought me for Christmas, so that a fresh loaf would be ready when the pasta was. The microwave pinged to announce that the milk for my hot chocolate was ready, so I filled up a large mug and squirted some cream on it.

Now I could snuggle on the sofa and watch something trashy. I used to love romcoms, back in the day, but when it turned out that *my* happily ever after wasn't as warm and tingly as the films suggested, I felt betrayed by them. They made me feel more depressed than usual these days. Obviously I didn't get much time to myself to watch films anymore, so I really wanted to treasure this slice of peace. None of my DVDs would suffice, so I rummaged through the box by the TV which contained dozens of the brothers' DVDs, settling for 'Django Unchained'. I had read a little about the slavery of America at school, so had an inkling of how the storyline went. 'Should I try and view in English?', I thought to myself. I knew very little of the English language, maybe sticking to my mother tongue would be more advisable.

I sipped on my hot drink, skimming the cream with my tongue as I watched the film.

I ate my pasta and bread as I watched another film.

I found an ice cream shoved at the back of my tiny freezer, and ate it as I watched another film.

It was getting late, and although I was enjoying the peace and quiet, I did worry about whether Thor was safe.

They eventually returned just before midnight, clearly intoxicated. I watched them as they staggered around the tiny flat.

"What?" Thor questioned aggressively.

"Where have you been?" I responded.

"I was out getting us both a job, just like you wanted!"

"Oh that's good then," I replied.

"Oh, is it? So glad you're happy then," he replied bitterly. "I'm going to be working in a bar, most evenings and weekends, so we'll hardly see each other!"

"Ok," I paused, not wanting to antagonise my inebriated partner further. "Well, it will do for now, eh?"

"Yes, it will. You got your wish!"

I paused again. "It's your wish too, you wanted the bigger home." There was an awkward silence. "There's pasta in the oven and bre…"

"We've already eaten," Kris piped up, sitting as close as possible to me on the sofa, nudging me with his rear.

"Oh, anything nice?" I responded, wondering how they had managed to afford a meal out.

Kris shrugged his shoulders as he grabbed the remote control from between us. He shuffled up a bit more, clearly wanting me to move. I did so gracefully, and proceeded to the kitchen to store the food that had been made. This took no more than a few minutes, but as

I poured myself a drink, I glanced over to the boys; Kris already had his feet up on the sofa and Thor was in my chair. I sighed, and departed to the bedroom, forgetting that the new bed covers needed to be put on. I sighed again, deciding to leave it for now, and curled up with the blanket that my grandma had crocheted for me years ago. Music on my phone and book in hand, I settled down again.

I must have dozed off, as I woke to find various bedcovers thrown in my direction. "REALLY?" Thor yelled, a little too loud.

"Shhh, we have neighbours."

"I DON'T GIVE A SHIT ABOUT THE NEIGHBOURS. IF YOU WANT TO CHANGE THE BEDSHEETS, AT LEAST HAVE THE DECENCY TO PUT THE CLEAN ONES ON."

"Ok," I whispered, "just give me a minute…"

"Don't bother now, do it tomorrow. I'm too tired to wait!"

He pulled the unsheathed duvet around him and rolled on his side, facing away from me. I put the book down, open at the last page that I read, pulled my earphones out and lay in the other direction, the sheets serving as a cover for me.

~

I awoke quite early on Sunday. The curtains were still open, as were the windows. It wasn't as warm as the day before and there was a chill enveloping me. Kristian sleeping in the living room meant that my daily activities were on hold until he was awake. Even the kettle or coffee machine would be too loud, and I had been reprimanded several times by the obnoxious flatmate. Thor was a much heavier sleeper, thank goodness, but all the same, I quietly sat up in bed and returned to my reading and listening. This didn't last long, as my mouth felt nasty from not brushing my teeth yet, and I was thirsty too.

Feeling minty, I emerged from my little bathroom and tiptoed to the kitchen. Kris was snoring loudly, one of his legs dangling from my tiny sofa. I stood silently at the counter. Opening one of my cupboards, I found an old box of lemon tea. I checked the expiry date, and gave it a little sniff. It seemed ok, so I retrieved a mug from the other cupboard, unplugged the kettle and tiptoed back to my bedroom.

Lemon tea was the hero of the hour. It tasted decent, would have been better if I hadn't just brushed my teeth, and I didn't even feel sluggish from the lack of caffeine – yet! Earphones back in and book opened, I sat in bed reading quietly until Thor roused.

What kind of mood would he be in, I wondered.

~

By my third cup of tea, I realised that it was almost midday, and Thor hadn't left for work yet. I didn't dare ruin his mood, though. We finished the fresh loaf of bread for breakfast, with a selection of jams in the fridge and I made a pot of coffee for the boys, to show a little truce.

We had started going on hikes on Sundays recently, but part of me just wanted to laze around the flat for a bit. As it seemed that the boys *weren't* going to work, I wasn't sure what would happen. I chose to not prompt anything. I showered and dressed, just in case we were to go out, but aimed to keep under their radar.

As it turned out, they both had a hangover, so chose to stay indoors anyway, although I was disheartened to see them both settle in front of the TV, and their gaming consoles. I returned to my bedroom, my book, and my lemon tea!

"When are we having dinner?" Kristian queried after entering the room unannounced.

I looked at my phone; it was just after 16:00. "I'll start shortly," I replied.

He huffed in frustration and punched my bedroom door. "Really? You are vandalising the flat because dinner doesn't arrive when demanded?!" I screamed at him.

"I'm fucking hungry!" he bellowed back.

"So? We won't get our deposit back when we move out if you continue to try to break stuff!" I explained.

He had already spilled various drinks and food on the floors, pasta thrown on the ceiling to *see if it sticks*, eggs thrown at the wall because *it's cool*, all causing irreparable damage. I was already resigned to the fact that we wouldn't get the deposit back anyway, but it still crushed me. We didn't have savings to pay for a deposit to a new place, so moving to a bigger place was just a pipedream. Hopefully, once he's out of the house more, we could focus on getting the place repaired enough to please the landlord, who was a friend of my mother.

I decided that I'd just start dinner now, to save the peace. As I passed the boys, I saw that Thor was looking at the property listings again. I sighed and continued into the kitchen. I prepped dinner with my back to them both, I was riled enough just listening to them, let alone having to watch the slobs that I had to feed. They both had huge appetites, so I had to choose cheap cuts of meat and fish, along with discounted vegetables. Today was hot dog waffles day. The boys loved it, and I enjoyed it on occasion, but every Sunday was a bit of a push for me. Nevertheless, I dutifully prepped the mix for the waffles from scratch and used our little griddle pan for the onions and smoked sausage. Both of the hobs in my tiny kitchen were working intensely.

I was used to hob-juggling now, and as I stared blankly at the food, I remembered how picky Kris was when he first moved in. Well, I say moved in – he simply didn't go home. This meant that he had lived in the same clothes for weeks – literally weeks! No showers. No washes. No teeth brushed. No clothes washed. For weeks! In the end, their father sent him some money to buy new clothes. Kris bought pyjamas and spent the rest on new games. I foolishly started doing his laundry on the day that he changed into his pyjamas, although he still never showered. In fact, the whole time he had lived here, I don't think he'd showered. I bought him a toothbrush, which was still in its packaging. I was resigned to the fact that the sofa would need to be cleaned thoroughly, or maybe even discarded, as he'd chosen to not put a sheet on it when he slept. The same applied to the cushions, with his greasy hair.

The first time that I'd cooked hot dog waffles, I'd included the obligatory fried onions. He threw his full plate of food at the kitchen cupboards. I looked at that cupboard now, door-less, and closed my eyes. Since that day, he had made a point of making sure that no vegetables were included with any meal, hovering over me as I plated the food.

Once ready, they scurried to their plates and returned to their gaming. I sat at the breakfast bar to eat mine. Maybe I'd eat in my little haven of a bedroom in future. I contemplated getting a TV for my room too, while I still had a little money of my own. When Thor had first moved in (again, it was a case of him not leaving one day), he had tried to micromanage my finances, wanting to know how much money I had received. He even wanted me to give him all the receipts, but I had stood my ground. It was my flat, my money. I knew that would change if we moved to a larger place. I'd contemplated changing jobs for a long time, and hoped to be receiving a higher wage than now, but know it'd take time. I wouldn't get a good reference from Hansen, in fact I wasn't sure if I wanted to stay in that type of work anymore. I certainly wouldn't reveal any wage increase to Thor. Such discretion probably wasn't a good way to have a relationship, but I didn't feel selfish.

After dinner, I washed the pots and prepped my lunch for tomorrow. Next, I set about writing my weekly *report of wrongdoings*, as I liked to call it, for Mrs Hansen. It had just been this Hanna that was of any significance this week, and there was very little to report, although I was pushed out of the office for most of Friday. What had they got up to, I wondered. I then realised that he, Hansen, was as badly behaved as the Valle brothers who resided with me. Sure, they weren't philandering arseholes (I hope!), but laziness and deceit seemed to be matching traits of them. Maybe it was all men? No, Pappa has never had any of these attributes, has he?

A shriek from Kristian brought me back into the room, a triumphant victory of whatever game they were playing. He danced around me in a childish manner, whooping loudly. At times it seemed like he was just a hyper 12-year-old. Maybe that's why his parents had kicked him out? It made me question if I ever wanted children of my own. He helped himself to a beer from the fridge, a beverage I never even knew existed. Maybe he did start his job yesterday and had been paid immediately? I didn't want to pry for now, while he was in a good mood. I reached into a cupboard and gingerly retrieved a bottle of wine I had managed to hide, grabbed a glass, and retreated to my room.

Chapter 3 – I'm in

Worry didn't fall upon me until the moment I set foot into the office building. I now feared what the day would hold for me; would Hansen have me back in the office? I enjoyed my Friday with Aggie, and I could now see how happy she was in her job. She was busy watering the plants when she caught sight of me and pulled a face. I laughed and she buzzed me in.

"Do you think these plants are looking greener, Line?" she piped up, enjoying her little rhymes.

"They look superb…" my brain was desperately scanning the alphabet. She knew I couldn't find anything to rhyme with Aggie, well, nothing complimentary, which tickled her all the more. "Zig-zaggie!" I concluded. We both burst into more laughter.

"Zig-zaggie?" Aggie repeated. "You really did try the whole alphabet, didn't you?"

I nodded in fake embarrassment. She laughed again.

"So, I had a note on my desk this morning from Mr Olsen. You are to be working with me this week."

"Hansen not coming in this week then?"

Aggie shook her head. "Apparently having some 'family issues'," she did the air quotes with her fingers.

"Oh, I guess it is something to do with Friday then," I surmised.

"I think I missed most of that once I was on the bus?"

"Oh yes, it totally kicked off. Hansen had to bundle her away into his car."

"How exciting! I shall have to start walking home!"

We settled into our morning activities. I still had some filing to do, but doubted that it would be enough to keep me busy for the whole week. I spent far more time watching Aggie performing her daily activities. Maybe something like this would be a good alternative job for me.

When I first went to college, I was hoping for a career in law, as the legal secretary I had become, but now I wasn't even aiming for a career, just a job that pays, that fulfils me. Aggie's job seemed to be just that, except it looked more complicated. I suppose a higher wage would require more skills. It was a world of wonder watching her whizz around doing many different tasks.

I slowly sorted the work I had, knowing that it wouldn't last me the whole week. I no longer had bi-daily trips to Marit's. I couldn't afford to buy anything from there. I had a tub of pasta and salad for my lunch today, and probably for the rest of the week – I had made an awful lot! Aggie was more of a sandwich kind of girl. I'd probably bake another loaf tonight to keep me in lunches for the rest of the week.

I offered to 'man' the reception whilst Aggie had her lunch in the kitchen. As I sat there, I realised that Aggie used to do this all of the time without my help, which made me feel a bit stupid, especially since she acted grateful for the assistance. Still, I did the job to the best of my ability. The post lady arrived and I buzzed her in, using the button under the desk. She handed over a large pile of letters, all different sizes. I had to sign for a parcel on an electrical device.

"Where's Agnes today?" the lady asked.

"Just having lunch in the kitchen," I replied, smiling politely.

"Ah, lovely, I'll be getting mine soon. Nearly finished for the day," she beamed.

"Ooh, how come you finish early?" I enquired curiously.

"I start at 5 a.m.," she explained.

"Blimey!" I exclaimed. "Do you enjoy it though?"

"It's ok. I've been doing it for years now, and it gets easier, especially when there are nice people like you and Agnes around. Everyone gets bad customers in their work, so you just take the rough with the smooth."

I nodded. "Well I'll be here with Aggie, I mean Agnes, all week. I'm Line."

"Hi, Line, I'm Nora," she responded, smiling and giving me a virtual handshake.

She was soft-spoken, despite her grand stature of at least six feet tall. I wouldn't say she was fat; stocky maybe. Her hair was white-blonde and cropped, and she wore her uniform with pride, donning the required grey shorts with multiple pockets on this warm summer day. Her bag was laden with parcels and letters of all sizes. She was clearly very busy and so she bid her goodbyes and carried on with the rest of her deliveries.

As she left, I noticed a figure dodge through the door before it could lock automatically. It was Hansen, who in turn held the door open for another: his wife. Sneaky little snake. Hansen blanked me completely and headed for the lift. Heidi attempted to approach me but was reprimanded by her husband like a disobedient dog. I had the 'Hanna report' ready for her but this was obviously not a suitable time. I became quite nervous and agitated just because Hansen was in the building. I busied myself with my work, hoping to complete it before he had finished in his office, but he re-emerged just a few minutes later.

"I heard the door buzz, Line, I assume it was Nora and hopefully not the Hansen or his Stepford Wife?!"

I was speechless and could feel the anxiety rise within me, as Aggie caught sight of the Hansens and quickly turned on her heel back into the kitchen.

"This place really is just the pits," Hansen hissed through gritted teeth. "Here's some work to be getting on with, Larsen." He threw some more random papers at me and promptly left.

"Just a moment, Kenneth," Heidi shouted to her husband. "I just need to speak to Miss Lars…"

"YOU WILL DO NO SUCH THING!" he bellowed at her, storming across the reception area to grab her.

I was worried that I was going to have to intervene if he hurt her, but she pulled her arm away and followed him out. I buzzed the door to let them out.

"It's ok, Aggie, they've gone now."

The kitchen door opened slightly. "I'll just give it a few minutes," she said, between heavy breaths.

I wasn't sure if they were from crying or laughing. She reappeared with a tissue in her hand, wiping her eyes, and it soon became apparent that it was the latter. We both continued laughing for a fair few minutes, while mimicking a Stepford Wife from the movies.

"No doubt I'll have Mr Olsen contacting me soon," she eventually said. "There's no way I can get out of this one, is there?" She laughed and pulled a face. We both laughed again.

My lunchtime was next, and I sat quietly and ate my cold pasta and salad. It wasn't something I could eat every day, so I decided that I would feed it to the boys later and make more bread for sandwiches tomorrow. I decided to use the money I was going to spend on tonight's dinner on something delicious from Marit's. On my way, I popped into the little delicatessen shop and picked up some spicy sausage to bring some new life to the pasta for later, and would do for tomorrow's sandwiches too. I'd stopped buying breakfast and lunch for them shortly after they had moved in, but was already in the habit of baking a loaf every evening, and there was plenty of cheese in the fridge.

The queue at Marit's was standard for this time of day. I persevered though, looking forward to a pastry and hot chocolate. I'd never really paid much attention to how much the pastries cost, but hoped to have enough for an extra pastry for Aggie. Soon I was in pole position and Marit started bagging up pastries.

"You're late today," she smiled at me.

"Hey, Marit, Hansen isn't in this week, so I won't be needing the pastries, so sorry."

"Oh, he was in not long ago, picking up a brunette..."

"Yeah, I think that was his wife. He popped in to give me some more work, but I'm working with Aggie, the lady on reception."

"Oh, I should have not ordered so many pastries..."

I felt terrible. "I'm so sorry, it took me by surprise, then I just got swept into the inertia for the day. I will be getting one or two, although I have no idea how much they cost."

I held my hand out to show her the change from the deli. "You can get four for that?" she suggested.

I really wanted the hot chocolate, but knew that it would be nicer for both Marit and Aggie if I took the pastries instead. I nodded and she allowed me to choose. I gave her the money and headed back to work.

We spent the rest of the afternoon eating pastries, drinking coffee and laughing. By the end of the day, I had managed to complete all of my work, and Aggie followed me out of the building and locked up.

"See you tomorrow, Line. Let's hope I don't screw up anymore today!" We both laughed. "Don't let the asshole brothers get you down. Spit in their food if they do! And make sure you have eaten vegetables before you do!"

"I'll mash some veggies into their food. See you, Aggie - you and Mr Olsen!" I laughed.

She pulled a face and headed for the bus stop. I stood and watched from a distance until she was safely on the bus. I was still a little wary about the stability of Heidi Hansen's mental state. I even held the 'Hanna report' in my hand in case she was to pounce on me on the way home. I waved at Aggie and she pulled another face.

I turned to walk home, still laughing, and bumped into Thor.

"Oof!" I exclaimed.

"Hello, Line," he smiled at me.

"Where are you going?" I asked, confused at his appearance.

"Work, of course," he grinned. "First night for both of us."

"Both of us?" I questioned, hoping he hadn't roped me into a second job.

"Yeah, me!" Kris shouted, rushing at me.

"Oh, cool, excellent. What time do you finish?"

"Keeping tabs on me already, Larsen?" Thor mocked me.

"No, just wondered when you would want dinner?"

"Ohh, just leave it in the oven or something. We won't be home till nearly midnight."

"O…Ok, I'll see you later or tomorrow then?"

He nodded and saluted me, leaning into me for a quick kiss. Kris attempted to copy his brother, but I stopped him in his tracks. Didn't need him invading my personal space!

Once home, I firstly made myself a hot chocolate. Next, I sat in *my* chair and watched *my* TV, drinking *my* hot chocolate. Then I scrubbed *my* sofa and dried it with a hairdryer, and double folded a sheet to tuck into the surface of sofa, with a blanket draped over the back. I took one of Thor's pillows and put a clean pillowcase on, then replaced the cushions so I could wash them. All dirty bedding was put on a hot wash, and clean bed sheets onto the bed. Thor's remaining pillow now had a clean, plain blue case on it, and I pushed my two pillows into the floral case that matched the curtains and duvet cover. I chilled out for the next few hours and ensured that I was in bed early enough that I wouldn't have to cross paths with the other flatmates.

Heidi Hansen

Chapter 4 – The Blood That Moves the Body

After sneaking out of the flat, I arrived at work early the next morning. With all work completed, I spent the morning sitting with Aggie, watching her fly through the chores effortlessly. First, she cleaned the reception area and watered the plants. The mail was sorted into the various shelves behind the desk, which she called 'pigeonholes', once Nora had arrived, and we had chatted to her for a few minutes. I felt like a spare part though, as she was always busy yet there was nothing I could do to help her. She seemed happy in her work though. She pulled faces when no one was around and we laughed, a lot!

Hansen and his wife arrived again, in the late morning. Hansen blanked Aggie and I, and Heidi seemed to know better than to attempt to talk to me. There did appear to be a bruise on her cheek, and another on her arm. The woman, who was in her mid-forties, had unkempt mousy-coloured hair, tied back into a simple ponytail. She was holding her husband's hand, or was he holding hers? I wasn't sure if she still wanted the infidelity reports, but I did observe the dirty look that we both received from her. I guessed that she was still angry following yesterday's mishap. They both entered the lift, and I breathed a sigh of relief.

"Now, Aggie, just so you know, Mr and Mrs Hansen are in the building!" I teased her and she pulled a face. "At least I'll be getting some more work now," I continued.

She decided to take this opportunity to go for her lunch break, and today she was meeting her husband for an anniversary lunch. My mind drifted to one of my favourite topics – food! I really wanted a hot chocolate, and pastries – I was clearly addicted. I wondered how I could generate the extra cash, as I only had my daily allowance for our dinner later. I was acutely aware that the only food we had at home was bread ingredients, cheese and the spicy sausage that I bought yesterday. Oooh, I could use the barbeque sauce that was tucked at the back of the cupboard and make pizza! My tummy rumbled in agreeance.

As if I had summoned him, Thor appeared at the door, and I buzzed him in.

"What are you doing here?" I smiled.

"Got a job interview!" he exclaimed excitedly.

"Wow, that's great! Where at and what job is it?"

"Here. Hansen's looking for an assistant manager-type role. Someone to look after the office when he's not in."

"Oh," I replied, slightly dreading the thought of working with him every day.

There was another tap at the door. It was Kris.

"I told him to come with me, then we can just go straight to work after – if I need to go back to that job, of course!"

I reluctantly buzzed his brother in, and Thor told him to sit in the reception area until the interview finished.

"Wish me luck?"

I smiled the best I could, and he headed for the lift.

Kristian sat on the chair for less than a couple of minutes before approaching me and bombarding me with random questions, like a hyper toddler. I tried to get him to go and sit down but he resisted. I didn't like to leave him unattended, so postponed my plan to make coffee and pulled my water bottle out of my bag, which was by my feet.

Mr Olsen appeared from the back door, indicating his office, "Work," he mouthed.

He disappeared into the room behind the reception desk. I was worried that Kristian's behaviour would alert Mr Olsen, which could reflect badly on me.

"What's Tweedledum doing here?" Aggie enquired, nodding in Kristian's direction, when she returned from her lunch.

I explained everything and she huffed. I laughed.

Mr Olsen emerged from his office, with a pile of paperwork in his hand.

"More work for me, sir?" Aggie saluted him.

He laughed. "No, I'm taking this home with me."

He disappeared out, same way he had come in.

"Did you want me to wait until the Hansens have all left?" I offered.

She shook her head. "I don't think any of these idiots could fight their way out of a paper bag!" she laughed and pulled a face.

"Ok, I won't be long anyway. I'm just going to Marit's for naughty pastries. Any preference?" I whispered, not wanting Kris hearing about my indulgences.

"Oooh! I'll have one of the raspberry ones please." She rummaged in her purse. "I'll have one of those hot chocolates too, please." She pushed some kroner notes into my hand.

I felt uncomfortable taking money from her as I wanted it to be my treat, but also knew that I couldn't afford that much.

"Ok, I'll be back in a flash."

Aggie acted out a Wonder Woman move and I laughed. She returned to her desk and spun around on her chair. She pressed her magic door-opening button and released me out into the world. I turned back to thank her, and she pulled a funny face. I could totally handle this new environment for a job, Aggie just made it fun.

I walked toward Marit's, popping into a grocery store on the way to pick up some chicken for today's dinner, which I'd make into a stir-fry, using the noodles that we already had in the kitchen cupboard, as I really didn't fancy spicy sausage. I could pop into the work fridge until it was time to go home. I was quite grateful that Aggie had given me some money. Marit's coffee shop was as busy as ever.

"How can you afford food from here if you are so skint?" a voice startled me.

"It's Aggie's treat," I replied to Kris, who was well within my personal space.

"Excellent, I'll have…"

"No, she doesn't have enough money for anything other than a couple of drinks and pastries." It was only a small white lie, I'd fill Aggie in just in case he mentioned it with her. "How did the interview go?" I asked Thor, who had caught up with his brother.

"It was quite an easy one. He's going to let me know by the end of the day. I'm pretty sure that the job is mine, plus I don't think he's interviewed anyone else, has he?" I shook my head, wanting to focus on my order as I was next in line. "We could definitely get the apartment that we looked at the other day," he continued.

I focused on Marit. "Two hot chocolates and two raspberry pastries, please."

"We only have one raspberry left," Marit replied.

"Oh, erm…I'll have that one then." I pointed to a swirly one.

I paid, and Kris grabbed the swirl pastry, passing half to his brother.

"Seeya later, after I finish work," Thor announced, spraying bits of flaky pastry at me. "It could be my last night there!" he continued.

"Well, don't quit just yet," I replied.

Marit placed the two drinks in a takeaway tray, and I made my way back to work.

As I arrived, I found Hansen at the door to the reception, holding it open.

"Larsen," he began, when he spotted me. "There's a couple of letters on the desk."

I nodded. 'I might need Aggie's help with that', I thought.

"Come on, Heidi," he shouted, breaking off our conversation briefly.

She appeared out of the ladies' toilet, trotting towards her husband.

"One letter is for you. You are sacked, and this last week is your final week. For gross misconduct on the Kari Nordmann case. You will receive no more work from me, and I have cleared your workload that was on your desk in reception. You can't be trusted with confidential information, and you are lucky that I'm not suing you for it. You WILL remain in the building, collecting mail, but

NOT opening it. You will continue answering the phone, but only to take a message, until I get the phones transferred to the new office. Yes, I'm moving my business away from this shitshow of a company. The other letter is for Mr Olsen, giving notice for the office too."

I was stunned. Heidi breezed past me, avoiding eye contact.

"Oh, and one more thing, Larsen, tell your boyfriend that I had no intention of hiring him. This was purely a fact-finding mission to find out exactly what you did during my absence."

And with that, they both left the building. I returned to the reception desk and stood holding my letter for a few moments, then opened it shakily. What would I do now? The letter said he would pay me for the rest of the week, 'as per our contract'. What would I do for money? I returned to my seat at the reception desk and placed the hot drinks and letter on my section of desk. I could see the letter for Mr Olsen, which was still sealed. I looked at the raspberry pastry that was still in my hand. I headed to the kitchen to get a plate for it, and to put the chicken in the fridge. The door was pulled closed, and I wondered why. I knocked and pushed it open.

"Aggie, are you decent?" I whispered.

I pushed the door open more and found Aggie on the floor.

"Holy shit, Aggie, are you ok?" I screeched, realising that the door wouldn't open as she was half-lying against it, so I stepped over her legs.

"Aggie, Aggie, Aggie?" I kept repeating myself, seeing if I could get a response.

It was then that I saw the blood. It was everywhere, pooling around her. Maybe she had fallen and bumped her head? No, it appeared to be coming from her back? I grabbed my phone out of my pocket and called for emergency services.

"Hello. Where's your emergency?" the operator asked.

"I...I... need someone. My friend is on the floor and has blood coming out of her. I think it's coming from her back."

"What's your name?"

"Line." I knelt down beside Aggie so that I could examine where the blood was coming from.

"And what's the name of your friend that's hurt?"

"Aggie... Agnes Johnsen." I leaned closer to her and touched her shoulder, gently whispering, "Aggie, are you ok? What happened?"

"Where are you right now?"

"I'm...we are in the kitchen at work." Still kneeling, I looked around the room for a sharp edge that she could have fallen onto.

"Where is work? What's the address?"

"Olsen Business Services," I replied. I could hear the operator tapping the address in.

"Is that at Kirkegata?" They asked.

"Y...yes, what do I do?"

"Can you see what is causing the blood loss?"

"She...she's laying on her side. I c...can't move her!"

"Is she breathing?"

I leaned over Aggie, trying not to touch or hurt her, shaking to my core. "I can't hear anything," I replied frantically.

My own breathing became irregular, almost as if I was to create oxygen around us to allow her to breathe.

I heard a loud bang at the main door. "I...I think they're here," I told the operator.

"Yes, I can confirm that they are at the premises now. I'm going to hang up the phone now, if you can let them in." I stopped the call and ran to the desk to press Aggie's button for the door.

I lead them to the kitchen, and they requested that I stay in the reception area so that I'd be out of the way. I sat in my chair and just sobbed. I could hear them saying her name and occasionally one of them asked me the occasional question, like her age, how long she had been there, but I didn't know. They told me that she had been stabbed with a knife, but that there was no knife there. Did I know where it was? I just sat in my chair, covered in my friend's blood, shaking.

The police arrived at some point, and asked if I would go with them to their station to answer some questions. I stared down at my hands, my friend's blood dripping from them, onto the desk and floor.

"Line," one of them spoke, "this lady here is going to take some photos of your hands and then we can clean them for you." I continued to stare down at my hands.

A lady flashed a lanyard at me with a laminate label hanging from it. She showed me how to hold my hands, and she took some photos.

"Try to keep them still, Line."

"We're going to take you to the station now," a young officer stated. "You can't wash your hands here, as it is a crime scene, but you can do it when we get there." He placed some paper towels over my hands and walked me to a police car. I sat in the back seat, and he walked around to the driver's seat.

"I want t…to to… be with Aggie. I need to look after her."

"I'm sorry, Line, I'm afraid that Agnes is dead."

The words rang out in my head, like someone was smashing my head with a bell.

I don't remember the car journey.

They walked me into the station and a few people turned round to look at me, look at the blood on me. I was shown where the toilets were, and I was to wash my hands and then strip off my clothes. A lady came in with me, to see if I had any wounds or blood beneath my bloody clothes. She bagged up my clothes and I stood there in my underwear, shivering; partly from shock and partly because I was cold. She said that I didn't need to remove my underwear and then she gave me some other clothes to wear. They weren't mine. Of course they weren't mine, I had been at work. Everything was just so confusing to me.

It felt like I was wrapped in cotton wool, or bubble wrap.

Voices were muffled.

People were blurred.

I was escorted into a room and given a drink of water in a plastic cup. A detective entered the room and sat opposite me.

"Hello, Line, my name is..." I didn't catch his name, but nodded anyway. "We have brought you in so that we can get a picture of what happened today."

I nodded. "Did she fall on a knife?" I asked.

He shook his head. "We haven't found a knife."

"I bought a pastry. There was meant to be two pastries, but my boyfriend's brother took one."

"Ok," the detective wrote it down. "Was your boyfriend's brother in the office with you? In the kitchen?"

I shook my head. "No, this was at Marit's."

"And who or what is Marit's?" he asked.

"C...coffee shop."

"Right," he wrote that down.

"M...maybe she was in kitchen getting plates for pastries, and maybe a knife to cut them up?" I remembered that she had done that yesterday so that *"it looks like there is more now"*.

I cried a little as I relayed this last bit of information. I grappled for my coat pocket to get a tissue and the pastry, before realising that they had taken my coat away. The detective pushed a box of tissues over to me.

"Did she fall on the knife?" I repeated.

"We couldn't find a knife at the scene," he replied.

I frowned. "Is it still inside her then?" I asked.

"No, we don't think she fell on a knife. It looks like someone has stabbed her."

"Someone?" I asked.

"Yes, so it looks like she has been murdered."

"Murder?"

"Yes."

"Aggie?"

"Yes."

"What about her husband?"

The detective wrote something down. "Her husband? Was he in the building?"

"No," I shook my head. "She had just been out on a lunch date with him. It was their... anniv..." I burst into tears. "What about her husband? Someone needs to tell him."

"Yes, we will track him down and let him know." He scribbled something on his notepad.

I could feel myself shaking and I opened my mouth to talk, but shut it again as I didn't know what to say. I started to feel very panicked, and my breathing became shallow, like someone was sitting on my chest. I could feel myself becoming dizzy, and I put my head down on the table to try and let it pass.

The detective opened the door and spoke to a colleague.

"Murdered?" I repeated, my head swimming.

The lady who had taken my clothes came in with a cup of tea. "Here's some hot, sweet tea."

"I don't like sweet…"

"It's for the shock. Sip it slowly and just breathe."

It was the worst tea I had ever had, so sipping it was definitely a good idea.

Once I had calmed down, they asked me to repeat what had happened, from when I had found Aggie.

"I was only out for a few minutes," I concluded.

Once I had recalled everything, they asked me what happened before I went to Marit's, but once Aggie had come back from her lunch date. She'd asked for hot chocolate and raspberry pastry. Gave me money… what had I missed?

A locum doctor arrived to assess my emotional and mental state, and gave me some sedatives to help me sleep. Eventually they took my fingerprints, thanked me for my time, and arranged for transport home. No one was home, so I just went to bed.

Chapter 5 – There's Never a Forever Thing

Despite the sedatives, I had a restless night, although I had cried myself to sleep. I woke up wrapped tightly in Thor's arms. He roused about the same time as I did. He embraced me just a little bit tighter and kissed my head.

"I heard what happened, Line," he whispered. "I'm so sorry. It must have been awful."

I cried for a long time, and he held me tight.

It was a given that I had no intention of going into work today, and this was confirmed in a telephone call from a very upset Mr Olsen. He said that the police had cordoned off the entire building and were processing evidence and talking to all clients that were in the building at the time of the attack. He gave me his sincerest condolences and I returned the sentiments, trying hard to control my emotions. He said he'd let Hansen know what had happened and confirm that I wouldn't be back in the office for the remainder of my notice period.

The rest of the day was a blur. Thor cancelled his evening's work so he could stay with me. He stripped the covers on the sofa and brought our duvet and my pillow in and settled me down snuggly on the sofa with a coffee and a roll of toilet paper. I cried and napped and was aware of the TV being on, although I paid no attention to it. I was offered food, but couldn't face anything. I was woken shortly before midnight, when Kris was banging around demanding to have the sofa to sleep, so I dragged my covers to bed.

~

I awoke the next day unsure of the time. It was the sound of raised voices that broke my deep sleep. I couldn't remember the last time

I had slept that deeply. It was obviously due to Aggie's death. There was a knock on my bedroom door.

"Hello?" I responded.

The door creaked open, and my father appeared.

"Pappa?" Was I dreaming still?

"Hello, Bumblebee," he replied.

He hadn't called me that for years.

He sat down on the bed. "How are you?" he asked.

I started crying and he hugged me tightly.

"Go and have a shower," he said finally, once I had composed myself a little. "Pack a few days' worth of clothes, you're coming home with me."

He kissed me on the head and proceeded to the living room. I gently rolled out of bed, and winced from the pain. I hurt, inside and out. I guessed it was from the stress of the previous day. Realising that there were no clean towels, I wandered into the living area to get one out of the dryer.

"WHILE SHE'S AWAY, YOU WILL SORT THIS FLAT OUT UNTIL IT IS AT LEAST PRESENTABLE. YOU WILL STOP TREATING MY DAUGHTER LIKE A SLAVE. YOU, KRISTIAN, WILL PUT YOUR BEDDING AWAY SOMEWHERE, EVERY DAY WHEN YOU GET UP."

"There is nowhere to pu..." Kris protested.

"YOU WILL FIND SOMEWHERE."

"We are looking for somewhere bigger to live, so that…"

"You will get yourself decent jobs and contribute to the expenses here *before* you consider getting a bigger place. If this place is too small for three of you, bring in enough income to be able to *afford* a bigger place. If you can't, then the extra person, Kristian, *must leave*."

I remained in the doorway, trying to think of a way to sneak past to get the towel.

"Line," my father addressed me, "are you ok?"

"I.. j… just need to get a clean towel," I explained.

Kris and Thor busied themselves, sorting out some of the mess. There was a pizza box thrown on the floor in the kitchen, and there were several beer cans on the surfaces. Coffee mugs from the last couple of days were in the sink. Coffee had been spilled on my chair, and it looked permanently stained with no effort to wipe up. The worst of it was that I was used to it.

I grabbed the last remaining clean towel, which was still slightly damp, and returned to the bathroom. I dressed and packed a few items of clothing, as instructed by Pappa. I returned to the living room and Thor passed me a cup of coffee and settled me onto a tidy sofa. He sat down next to me and asked me how I was. Pappa remained in the kitchen, visually supervising Kristian's tasks.

"Come on then, Line, we need to go now, there's a flight soon."

I stood up, and Thor took my mug from me. "Wash this up when you're done, Kris," he said, putting it on the breakfast bar and nodding at it.

Kris opened his mouth to speak, but Pappa glared at him. Thor hugged me and kissed me on my head. Pappa held the door open for me and took my bag from me. I checked my rucksack bag for my phone, then closed the door behind me. There was a taxi waiting outside and we were soon whisked away to the airport.

The whole plane journey was a blur. Back in Bergen, my hometown, my big sister, Lillianne was waiting for us, to give us a lift to my parents' house. She embraced me so fiercely, I thought I would break. We were home in a flash, and I soon had a hot drink in my hand.

"We were so worried that it was you," Lilli blurted, close to tears. "We heard about a violent attack at Olsen's on the news. I tried your phone a few times, but it kept going to answer machine."

"I haven't even looked at my phone since it happened," I admitted. "Once the police arrived, they took me to the station to question me."

I pulled it out of my bag and saw so many missed calls.

"I contacted Belle, and she hadn't even heard about the... it," she continued. "She went straight to the offices to check, and the police wouldn't help her, as your colleague's family hadn't been informed. I tried to call Thorfinn, but he didn't answer his phone either. Then Belle called me back. Apparently, she caught sight of you being put in the police car. I was relieved, although we didn't know how serious the attack had been, but was sure that any attack on you would mean they'd put you in an ambulance rather than a police car, so I knew you were ok, relatively speaking."

"Murdered," I exclaimed. "I just can't..."

"It's so scary, sis. It could have been..."

Pappa put a hand on Lilli's knee and hushed her. "Shhh. Let's not think about that, Lillianne."

"Did you know her well?" she asked.

I nodded. "Very well. She was amazing. She worked on the reception desk, and I had been working at the desk too over the last couple of days; my boss told me to."

Lilli reached over and squeezed my hand. We sat quietly for a few minutes, and I found myself thinking about every single detail from yesterday.

"Am I allowed to be here?" I asked Pappa, suddenly realising that I could have been a suspect.

He nodded. "I rang the police during the flight to Oslo this morning. They didn't want to tell me, as I could have been anyone, so I popped into the station to show them my ID before I went to your place. They said you were only a person of interest because you found her and because you worked there, but not really a serious suspect. More like eliminating you from their enquiries, I guess."

"Most of it is just a blur, but seeing her, all the blood, that is so clear."

"Don't think about it right now, you are here to relax. We are here to wait on you hand and foot."

I tried to smile, but just couldn't. My brain felt totally scrambled. I put my head back on the back cushion of the sofa and closed my eyes.

~

I awoke to the feeling of someone touching one of my feet. I jolted as a natural reaction and Lilli giggled.

"Knew that would wake you up!" she stated. I smiled. "Dinner is nearly ready," she continued.

"I don't feel hungry at all," I replied.

"It's your favourite, so I'm sure just a little would be appreciated?"

I nodded politely and walked over to the dinner table. Pappa walked in with a dish of meat cakes with mashed potatoes and cabbage. On any normal day I would have devoured the whole plateful, but I had no appetite and struggled to even look at it. All I could think of was all of the blood around Aggie, and the outward breath that she had exhaled. Was this the moment that she had died? Had I witnessed her literal last breath? Tears welled in my eyes again and I excused myself to go to the bathroom. I feared that I wouldn't make it to the bathroom when my legs began to feel weak, too weak to carry me. I stood by a nearby table to steady myself for a moment, until I felt I could move further. I lay on the floor once I reached the bathroom, and sobbed quietly. Once re-composed, I ventured to the sofa, curled up into a ball and fell asleep.

Chapter 6 – Lifelines

Sometime during the evening or night, someone roused me to take a sedative and then Pappa gathered me in his arms and took me to bed. I remained there for the majority of the next day. Pappa and Lillianne visited me various times to ensure I was ok and that I had everything I needed. I made an effort to join them for dinner. Pappa joked that I was going to have the meat cakes from yesterday. Instead, he gave me a small bowl of chicken soup with some freshly made bread.

"Just a little food should make you feel a bit better," Pappa explained. "If you want more, there's plenty left. No pressure, though."

The soup was delicious, and I just sipped it a little at a time. I managed a crust of one slice of bread.

"I'll keep it in the slow cooker and you can help yourself if you need any more," Pappa explained.

After dinner, Catrine Bystrom stopped by. She gave me a huge hug. We didn't really interact until last Christmas, and even that was brief.

"I was so worried about you. I heard about a murder, and then Pappa Filip told me that it was your workplace, and I was worried that it was you. I'm so relieved, although I'm sure it's not ideal to be faced with her... her body." I shuddered, Aggie's image flashing across my eyelids when I blinked.

I breathed deeply.

"Sorry, I don't want to bring it all up again," she continued.

We chatted for quite a while; about her; her job; her mother. Pappa gave her some soup and bread. She loved his soup, apparently.

"My favourite is his leek and potato," she told us both.

I smiled. I remembered a few occasions when we had eaten leek and potato soup, and it instantly took me back to my childhood. I recalled a time when the snow was so high that we couldn't get outside to make snowmen. I was around six or seven, Lilli would have been eight or nine. Catrine was there too, she would have been about 10, I think. We'd sat and slurped the soup, dunking bread into it. We'd all seen a film on TV that week, which showed a kid eating bread and soup like this, and we wanted to be just like that kid. It was the first time we had dunked, but it wasn't the last. I didn't recollect many times that I had spent time with Catrine as a child but realised that I probably had.

Pappa made us both hot chocolates, with whipped cream and marshmallows. Then some cupcakes appeared. I couldn't quite manage any, and I was getting rather fatigued. Catrine, laden with a small bag of cupcakes, made her way home.

I relaxed in the living room with Pappa. It was very calm and serene. Lillianne was out for the night, visiting her boyfriend, Bryn. Mamma worked away during the week, and would be home tomorrow. I enjoyed this quiet time with Pappa.

However, the peace was disturbed by a knock on the door. Pappa smiled and stood up to answer it. As he returned, he was followed by Mr and Mrs Valle, Thor and Kris' parents. I sat up straight on the sofa, allowing them to sit down.

"What's the matter, child, are you ill?" Mrs Valle enquired.

"N…no," I replied. "My work colleague was murdered, and I found her body."

"Yes, I am aware of that, but surely that is no reason to abandon your partner and his brother. They have had to borrow money from us as they have no food in the place."

I was taken aback by this. I had been so protected since I had returned to Bergen that I had expected it from them too.

"They both have jobs now. They are working in bars, and getting paid per shift," I explained.

"You still have duties with Finn and Kristian, you swore you would look after them."

"I did no such thing," I responded, getting agitated. "Both of them simply turned up at my place, at different points and then just didn't go home. That's why they both kept borrowing money for new clothes. And that was because I couldn't bear the smell that Kristian emitted after several weeks of living, and sleeping, in the same clothes. I may even have to get a new sofa since he has almost destroy…"

"How DARE you talk about my sons like that!"

I was ready for an argument, but Pappa intervened.

"It was my decision to bring Line home for a few days. She needed to recover from the shock of what happened."

"People die every day," Mr Valle piped up.

"Yes, they do, Dagfinn," Pappa responded, "But they don't get murdered in the same building that you work in, and they don't find the body! My daughter needed to get away from Oslo for a few days, for some recuperation…"

"Are you a doctor, Filip?" Mr Valle interrupted.

"Are you, Dagfinn?" he retaliated. "Line is my daughter, so my responsibility. Your sons are YOUR responsibility. And furthermore, when I arrived at Line's home to collect her, the place was a total mess. Beer cans, pizza boxes, dirty clothes strewn everywhere."

"Well, maybe they should move out and leave Line alone again?"

This sounded perfect to me.

"Maybe they should," Pappa replied, standing up to indicate that it was time for them to leave.

I realised that I should probably check my phone and see if there were any urgent messages for me. I knew that Pappa had asked the police to contact him if they needed anything, so it would just be friends and relatives. I pulled it out of my bag, which was laying at my feet where I had left it.

Two calls and three text messages from Belle. Three calls from Thor, and 10 texts.

I addressed the messages left on my answer machine.

"Hi Line, just checking you are ok? Heard what happened at your work today, just checking it's not you that was... was... hurt. Call me back as soon as possible, please."

"Hey, I still haven't heard from you and need to know you are ok? You have my number." That was Isabella too.

I braced myself for Thor's messages.

"Hey, Line, just checking that the flight was ok and you got to your parents' house safely. Call me back when you can. Love you."

I felt warm inside and smiled.

"Line? Where are you?"

"Why are you not answering my calls? It's the least you can do, surely?"

My smile disappeared. Time to check the texts. I started chronologically, and with Thor's.

'Hey sweetie. Hpe u r doin ok U shd be @ airport by now No u dont like planes. Let me no when ur @ ur parents'.

'R U there yet????'.

'Where r u?'.

'WTF is goin on???'.

'WTF. We havent got N E food???!!!'.

'WHY R U GHOSTING ME??'.

'DID U EVEN GO BAK 2 BERGEN???'.

'WTF'.

'Call me!'.

'Srsly, how long r u stayn there???'.

I exhaled deeply. I stood up and walked around the house to calm down. Pappa was in the kitchen, baking.

"Mmmm smells lovely!" I praised, hugging him from behind.

"Oh, hello, Bumblebee. I decided to do some stress-baking. I've never liked the Valles."

"I'm so sorry, Pappa," my voice wobbled a bit, and squeezed him tighter.

"No, no, it's not your fault. Like your housemates, they are responsible for their behaviour, and it's clear where their children inherited those traits."

"It's… I'm just sorry for bringing this to your home."

He turned round and shoved a freshly baked cookie in my mouth. I let my hold go to ensure it didn't drop onto the floor, and Pappa filled a glass with some milk for me.

"Mmmmm," was all I could say, and I sat down at the little table next to me.

A plate of different cookies appeared in front of me, and I devoured several.

"Did you get all your correspondence sorted?" he enquired.

"Almost," I replied. "I listened to Belle and Thor's voicemails, and have read his texts. I decided I needed to leave it there for a few minutes." I pulled my phone out of my pocket. "I'll read Belle's texts now and reply to her. I'm leaving Thor for now – let him stew!"

"Quite right too!" he nodded.

He returned to his baking and I stepped outside to walk around the garden for a bit.

'Hey, Leenaarrrr, hope you are ok? I heard about the incident at your work. Just checking you are ok? If you need anything, just let me know'.

'Just spoke to Lilli, and she says she hasn't heard from you either. Says she's going to get Pappa Filip to come and see you. Message me when you can. Xxx'.

She had always called my father Pappa Filip. Growing up with Isabella had been great. We had never had any falling outs, just a good, solid relationship. I think he had allowed my friends to call him by his name as a retaliation to when he was a teacher, when students had to call him Mr Larsen.

The evening air was only a little chilly. I wrapped my arms around each other to keep them warm as I had left my jumper in the house. I sat on one of the outside chairs and closed my eyes.

I replayed the whole day in my mind, looking for answers. There were a couple of business owners that came and went during the day. Only one of them stopped to talk to Aggie and he was just collecting mail. Hansen had come in with Heidi, then Thor and Kris. I went to Marit's and Thor and Kris were there, behind me. I went back to the office, and Hansen was outside, holding the door open, telling me about the letter that was sacking me.

I stood up and went back into the house, aiming for my bag in the living room. The letter was still in there, unopened. I sat down and ripped open the envelope. It was a short, hand-written letter on cheap, white, headed paper.

Dear Miss Larsen,

I am writing to you to inform you that as of today, 27th June, I no longer require your services and duly give you one week's notice.

Regards

H Hansen

What was I going to do now? We were struggling to make ends meet as it was, but without my income, we wouldn't be able to afford to live. I shoved the letter into my pocket, and I picked my mobile up to read and reply to my messages. I felt so down, so I thought I'd reply to Thor first.

'Hey. So sorry, I've just been completely knocked off my feet. Must be those sedatives! I'm doing ok, and will be home very soon. There's some pasta and rice in the cupboard. Anything else, you will have to use your own money for now. Speak soon. L x'.

I quickly started to write a reply to Belle, hoping to send before Thor responded. I looked at the time, it was early evening so hopefully he and Kristian would both be at work. I decided to call Belle rather than text, which also meant that I wouldn't miss a text reply from her, and my phone would be tied up if Thor did try to reply.

"Line, oh, Line, I've been so worried!" Belle answered, almost distraught.

"Hi, Bella," I replied. "I'm so sorry I've been unreachable. Pappa brought me to Bergen for a few days."

"I'm just so glad you are ok," she replied. "What happened?"

I explained the details of what had happened, trying hard to keep my voice steady.

"Do they know who did it?"

"The police? No, not as far as I am aware. Pappa told them to contact him if they need me."

"How long are you there for?" she asked.

"I'm not sure. I feel slightly less of a zombie now. I've been given some sedatives, which are working a treat."

"Ok, hun, I'm just glad you are ok," she repeated.

"Thor kicked off a bit about it."

"Why?"

"Because I wasn't answering messages. Even sent his parents round here, which was awful because they kept having a go at me, and Pappa!"

"How dare they upset you guys!"

"Yeah… he kinda kicked them out though."

Belle laughed. "Good old Pappa Filip!"

At this moment, Pappa entered the room so I said my goodbyes.

"I'm having some of the soup for supper, did you want any, sweetheart?"

My tummy rumbled loudly and we both laughed. I nodded, switched my phone off and followed him into the kitchen. He served up two bowls and brought over some bread.

"I'm not letting you go until you are eating better," he said, half-joking.

"Judging by the dire situation at the flat, there's no food there, so maybe I'd be better off not having an appetite."

"They're earning now, aren't they?" he enquired.

"Yes, but they seem to be starving, apparently..."

"Shame!" he chuckled, popping more bread into his mouth.

I smiled. "I got sacked," I announced.

Pappa dropped his bread. "WHAT?! When was this?"

"On the day of the murder," I explained. I thought for a moment. "Actually, I think my boss handed me the letter within minutes of Aggie getting... stabbed..." I frowned.

"How much notice did your boss give you?"

I pulled the letter out of my pocket. "A week, I think." He shook his head in disgust.

"The police have said that the building won't be accessible for the rest of this week," he confirmed, "so I guess that you won't be back there then?"

I shrugged.

"Probably a good thing, though?"

I nodded. We ate the rest of the supper in silence.

Heidi Hansen

Chapter 7 - Bumblebee

When I awoke the next morning, I padded in my slippers down the stairs and into the kitchen. If Pappa was required for anything, he was usually found in the kitchen; it was his favourite room in the house. Indeed, that was where I found him, along with my mother.

"Hello, Line. I've heard everything that has happened. I'm sorry for your loss."

Mamma was always very professional, very cold. She showed affection through monetary donations rather than hugs.

"Good morning, Bumblebee," Pappa greeted me, with a hot cup of coffee.

"Thanks, Pappa. How long did I sleep for?"

"About 14 hours, I think," he replied.

"WOW, those sedatives sure do knock you out!"

This, unfortunately, kicked Mamma into action, as a pharmaceutical rep, and she was wanting to know all about these meds. I handed her the box, and she accepted as if it was a Christmas present!

"Depending on the level of the impact of the event, you may need to continue taking these for a while. They'll probably allocate a psychologist for you to visit, who can decide whether these need to be ongoing. Maybe the psychologist will lower the dose so that you can function. Of course, it may also be the shock of the event that has caused you to sleep this much too…"

I switched off after a while, just nodding to appease her. Pappa rolled his eyes at me and I smiled. We were used to all this. He refilled my coffee cup, and brought out a massive bowl of fruit salad, with yogurts and granola for us to graze on.

"I see you have your appetite back," a voice behind me spoke as I filled up my bowl with seconds.

It was Lilli, who had arrived with Bryn, a tall, well-built bear of a man, with deep brown eyes and matching hair; anyone would feel safe in his arms. I knew Bryn quite well, as their relationship had been ongoing for a few years now. I stood up and gave them both a hug. Pappa pulled out a couple more bowls and mugs from the dishwasher and the new arrivals tucked in. Pappa made a fresh pot of coffee and placed it on the table, smiling.

"I love it when all of the family are here together."

"What will you do when we all move out?" I asked. He shrugged.

We all sat silent for a few minutes, apart from the sound of cutlery clinking crockery.

"I assume you will need to be back at work on Monday?" Mamma enquired.

I didn't want her to know that I'd been sacked, and neither did Pappa. We both knew that her reaction would be... well, stifling, I guess. She'd lecture, want to know why I'd had been fired, taking the side of Hansen rather than me.

"How about a nice hike this afternoon?" Pappa suggested, changing the subject.

"Wonderful, dear," Mamma replied.

"Great, I shall make some food to take with us," he offered.

I struggled more than the others during the hike. My reasoning was that I always suffered during hot weather. Pappa added that it could be the sedatives. Mamma just believed I was out of practice. Either way, I admitted defeat and sat down near a tree. I knew that they would come back down this way, so Pappa left the food bag with me. I pulled my phone out of my bag and switched it on. A barrage of messages came through, which took several minutes to complete. I closed my eyes whilst waiting, nervous to open them to see what was coming my way.

I levelled my breathing, in through the nose and out through my mouth a few times and then looked. Nothing from Thor. One text from Bella and one from Astrid. Bella's was just a simple 'take as long as you need xx'; Astrid's was more detailed, saying that she had spoken to Belle and was happy to hear that it wasn't me that had been hurt. I sent a quick text back to her, thanking her.

I lay back on the grass, waiting for my family to return. Remembering to bring my jumper, I then found that I didn't need it, so I rolled it up and put it under my head as a pillow. I hoped to rest my mind, but my brain kept going over the details of the day of the murder. I tried to work my way back, from when I found Aggie. Did I hear anyone running away from the scene? I scrunched my face up. No, there was no one about at all. What about when I first re-entered the building? The Hansens! I sat bolt upright. Heidi was in the bathroom and Hansen was waiting for her at the door. Why was she in the bathroom? Washing blood off her hands?

I felt a panic attack rising in me, I struggled to breathe. Why didn't I work this out sooner? She had attacked her just a few months ago. She was definitely unstable. I scanned my brain for other memories. 'Ah! Aggie mentioned something along the lines of them being weird or something, and then realised that they were there!'. It must be Heidi Hansen! She was originally the client, but I will now investigate her for the murder too.

It was time for me to return to Oslo. To get justice for Aggie and to sort out my life there.

Heidi Hansen

Chapter 8 - Shadowside

I awoke earlier than usual, but only slightly less groggy than the other days. Pappa had booked me a flight back to Oslo, when we had discussed this in more detail. We had shared a lovely dinner around the table, salmon being the main course. I'd not had salmon for a very long time, it wasn't something that the boys liked, which was a shame as it was relatively cheap. I had savoured every mouthful.

Now it was time to brace myself, I would have to face police, the Hansens, Thor and Kris. I wasn't sure which would be first.

There was fresh coffee in the pot, and I helped myself to a cupful while my parents busied themselves. Mamma was going back to Oslo too, but we wouldn't be seated together as her ticket was booked further in advance. She was also in Business Class! The fruit salad bowl had been replenished, and there was bread and many jams too. I'd need to have a weigh-in with my cabin case at this rate!

"How much space do you have in your luggage, Line?" Pappa interrupted my thoughts.

"Erm… a little…"

"Great!" He walked to the freezer and fished out several tubs of food. "There's some meat cakes in this one, and this one," he stacked the tubs onto the table, "has some salmon in it, just what was left over from yesterday. And this one…" he handed this to me directly, "is the chicken soup. When you want any of these, just heat it up in the microwave. You have had more than enough training on how to reheat," he chuckled.

"And this…" Mamma appeared from her home office, "is some money for you: to pay for a taxi from the airport, to cover you until you get a job, to use if you need a deposit for a new place, to come home if you need to." I frowned. "Your father told me."

It was an envelope with a wad of money in it. I tried to decline but knew this was impossible.

"Thanks, Mamma," I replied, when she shoved it back into my hand.

"Keep it in a *safe* place!" she insisted.

Pappa produced a thermal bag and stacked all the tubs in it. I fetched my belongings from my bedroom and returned to the kitchen. Opening my case on the counter, Pappa squeezed the bag in there.

"Good job it's just a domestic flight," he laughed, pushing the top down to zip it shut.

Lillianne had emerged from her bedroom and was eating breakfast. I sat down briefly and had another cup of coffee.

"You'll be awake all night with all that caffeine," Mamma tutted. "Come on, the taxi will be here in a couple of minutes."

I stood up and Lilli gave me a big hug. Pappa walked over and squeezed me tight. "If you need *anything*, just let me know," he whispered in my ear. I nodded.

"The car is here, Line," Mamma prompted me, and we both left.

In the airport lounge, we briefly spoke until it was time to board the plane. She reiterated that I could contact them whenever I needed to, then she whisked away to her seat, leaving me waiting to board.

As we approached Oslo, my anxiety started to kick in. I saw Mamma briefly, just as she alighted the plane; we caught each other's eyes and she nodded. Once through all the checks, I proceeded to a taxi rank and headed for the flat.

Chapter 9 – Scoundrel Days

As I opened the front door, I was greeted with a sight almost as shocking as finding Aggie. There were multiple people crammed into the living area, fairly rowdy, as it appeared they were all watching or playing video games. The first smell that hit me was marijuana, and then smoke, all mingling with body odour. I stood at the door for a few minutes, not quite knowing where to start. Thor was sitting on the sofa, and he was one of the gamers. Next to him was an unknown youth, male, who was also playing the same game. I retrieved my phone and clicked the icon to record it all. My favourite chair had been moved from its usual place and was pulled up close to the TV, and in it sat another male youth, who was drinking beer out of a can. He finished the contents and crushed it before throwing it on the floor. It was only then that anyone had realised that I was there, and he nudged Thor.

"Hey, dude, think the stripper has arrived!" He laughed.

"Hang on a mo, mate, can't stop right now!"

I left the flat and ventured downstairs to the main fuse box and switched all the electrics off. An abundance of shouting began, with Thor raging loudly. As I returned, there were multiple cans being thrown around. Thor stood up and saw me in the doorway. I assumed, foolishly, that he would tell everyone to leave and apologise. Not that he would storm toward me and reprimand *me* for *my* actions. He faced up to me in an aggressive manner, waving his arms like he wanted a fight.

"What the HELL are you doing? I was halfway through a game! You have let all of these people down, now we'll have to start a new game now!"

"No, you will not!" I retorted. "This is my place, not yours!" He walked towards me, and I backed away until my back was against the door. "Get everyone out! NOW!"

I stormed to my room for some sanctuary, only to find that Kris was in my bed, having sex with a girl that didn't even look old enough.

I screeched in frustration and disgust, dragging my suitcase back out into the living room. "Get everyone out, and change those bed covers!"

I stormed out of the flat and sat downstairs on a crate that was positioned next to the door. I figured that I would sit there until all of their friends had left. I waited, and waited, but there was no sign of movement. I walked back upstairs and put my ear to the door. There was chanting and cheering. It was only 11:00 and there were multiple drunk people in my home.

I searched my bag for my phone, and then my pockets, finding it my jeans back pocket. Who could I call? Who could help me in this situation? I walked back to the crate, sat down and just stared at my phone. I decided to first try Isabella, who answered almost immediately.

"Hi, Line, how are you doing?" she enquired.

"Ok."

"Are you still in Bergen?"

I shook my head. "No, I just got back to my flat. The place is a tip and there's loads of people there, all partying; playing games and drinking."

"Oh no!" Bella replied. "Do you want to come round here for a bit?"

"Do you mind, Belle?" I fought back tears.

"Of course I don't mind, silly head!"

"Thanks, I'll call a taxi now."

"I'll come and get you!" she insisted.

She arrived swiftly and I climbed into the passenger seat. On the journey back to Isabella's place, I told her all that had happened since I got back. She was disgusted about it.

Her apartment was so much nicer than my place. It looked more modern, with minimalist black furniture. We sat and drank a bottle of wine, which she had opened as soon as we arrived. We chatted, about what had happened with Aggie, about my stay in Bergen, about Bella's job.

"I wish I had somewhere here that you could sleep," she said. "As you can see, my sofa looks stylish but is totally uncomfortable to sleep on. I fell asleep here the other week and woke up in agony!"

I shook my head. "No, I'd never ask that!" I exclaimed. "If I've learned anything, it's so much better to live alone." I laughed bitterly.

"Is that what you are going to do then? Get them to move out?"

I pondered for a few seconds, then nodded. "Yeah, I think I am."

She topped up our glasses. "Here's to living alone!" she toasted, and we tapped our glasses together.

The drinking continued well into the late night, and I realised that Bella was getting tired.

"I should probably go, Tinkerbell," I suggested.

She looked at her watch and groaned. "WOW, it's way too close to Monday!" she exclaimed.

"At least you have a job," I replied.

She nodded. "What are you going to do?" she asked. I shrugged.

"I guess I'll figure that out soon, let's just focus on the flat for now, hey?"

She nodded again and hugged me. I booked a taxi and left as quietly as I could. It had been a very long drinking session with virtually no food, but luckily I had some of the snacks that Pappa had packed for me. When the taxi driver arrived, I said my goodbyes and got into the car.

As we arrived at the flat, I paid the fee and asked the driver to stay for a bit. I climbed the stairs and unlocked the door. There was nobody indoors, luckily. I gestured a thumbs-up to the driver. He nodded and drove off.

The flat still smelled awful, so I opened all of the windows. I stood by the sofa and assessed the destruction. It was like a disaster had occurred. Fast food packages were strewn around the whole living space. One of the curtains were hanging by a thread. There was drink spilled all over the sofa, some areas still wet, and I found the same on the carpet. My chair had been knocked over and one of my cushions was missing. I walked over to the kitchen, stepping over something that was either food that had been dropped or vomit. Cups were stacked in the sink, along with extinguished cigarettes. The coffee pot had been smashed onto the floor. An almost full milk carton was left out with its lid off, and a quick sniff confirmed that it wasn't drinkable.

I ventured over to the cleaning cupboard to get some rubbish bags, and then stopped. 'No, I'm not going to clean up after them anymore!' I thought to myself. I stepped back over the mess, grabbed clean bedding, which was still in the dryer from when I'd washed it last week, and aimed for my bedroom. I was apprehensive about this, as all I could vision was Kris in there with that girl. I tried to avoid looking at the bed and headed for the window. I opened the curtains and window. Turning back to the bed, I started stripping it, folding it up by the edges to avoid touching as much 'debris' as possible, and dumped it all in my laundry basket. I had intentionally thrown the duvet and pillows in there, I wanted a 'fresh' bed. I sprayed the mattress with laundry freshener and turned it over, rotating it at the same time. I had some spare pillows at the top of my closet, so I retrieved them and replaced the pillowcases. I had a blanket bundled up with the clean bedding, so that could replace the duvet. Sheets were changed and then the laundry basket was taken to the washing machine.

I returned to the kitchen, opened up my case and stacked my food tubs into the freezer, except one containing a soup, which I popped into the microwave. The rest of the stuff in my suitcase was dirty clothes so I shoved it all into the washing machine. I grabbed my chair and took it into my bedroom, along with my soup. The kettle and lemon teabags were still in my room, so I filled the kettle using my bathroom tap and switched it on. I swilled my cup in the sink, and gave it a little scrub, sniffing it to check it was ok. Now I could sit and think.

I plugged my earphones in to listen to music and sipped my soup. I mulled over the issues in my life; work, the flat, Bergen and the 'boys'.

I decided that I had stopped loving the flat, so decided to give notice to the landlord. I had just enough money to cover the rent for the next two months, the required notice period, plus enough money to feed myself.

Having no work to go to yet, money would become tight, so the Valles would *have* to chip in. I'd give them the option to pay some money and then buy their own meals, or pay more and we could save a little money with bulk food buying – which was what I had been doing up until this point. If there was an argument about the amount they'd pay, I could always reduce the bills by cancelling the broadband service, only having hot water when they weren't around, and so on. I'd assess the situation once we got a chance to discuss, which would probably be tomorrow. I pulled my planner out of my bag, and started to write down how much everything would cost, and then divided it by three. This, in theory would be how much we'd each pay, until the two months was up. What I would do after this would depend on when and where the work situation would go.

I would leave it a few days before even thinking about getting a job. My mother had given me that luxury by giving me some money, and therefore allowed me time to decide whether I would continue down the law secretary route, or find a completely different career. That could mean that I'd have to retrain at college, which I couldn't afford to do, unless it was included within a new job. If that was the case, I could be paid at a lower rate than I was receiving with Hansen. Again, I had the money that Mamma had given me, if needed.

The final quandary was whether I would stay in Oslo or move back to Bergen. This wasn't really a choice, or even considered until I had spent the time at home with my parents. It would almost be a case of choosing my parents and Lillianne versus Belle and my other friends. Family or friends essentially. Maybe I could research both locations for work? I decided to put this on a backburner for now.

Once I had finished my soup, I changed into some clean pyjamas and stored my bag (with my money in the zipped front pocket) in my closet. I took my sedatives and settled down for the night, hoping to not have to deal with Thor until tomorrow.

<u>Chapter 10 – I Wish I Cared</u>

I woke up quite late, around 10:30. Thor was sprawled out on his side of the bed, with one foot dangling out of the covers. I really didn't want him to dirty my fresh linen, but knew it was too late to worry about it now. I took a shower and put clean clothes on. I made a point of not being quiet, and brewed a pot of coffee in the kitchen. Kris shouted for me to be quiet; I ignored him. I returned to the bedroom and brought my mug and bag out. I sat at the breakfast bar and pulled out my planner from my bag to refresh my memory about last night's calculations. I started rewriting the calculations and options onto a fresh sheet of paper, using one side for the shared costs and the other side for if they chose to buy their own food.

Thor appeared just as I was filling my mug up with coffee, but I made no effort to pour him one. He stood still, watching me not make him a coffee, then leaned over to give me a kiss. I turned my head away.

"Good morning, beautiful. Glad to have you back," he said.

"Are you both at work today?" I said, ignoring his previous statement.

"No, we have Mondays off, why?"

"You can both get this flat clean," I replied. "Then we are going to talk."

"Are you at work today?" he asked.

"No."

"Fair enough, I don't know if the office building is released by the police yet anyway," he explained. I nodded knowingly.

"I'll probably be in the bedroom for most of the day." I announced.

Kristian started stirring. He stretched, groaned and farted. I shuddered internally. I certainly wouldn't miss him!

"You up for a game of..."

I stopped him on his tracks. "No, he isn't. There'll be no playing anything until this place is cleaned up and we have talked about all this."

"All what?" he questioned.

I waved my hand over the mess of the place. "What I witnessed when I came home yesterday, for a start."

"You should have told us when you were com..."

"NO! I should not need to give notice before coming back to my own home! Like I said, we'll sort that out once the place is decent enough."

"Whatever!" he sighed, laying back down and pulling the cover back over him.

I entered the living area and approached the TV. I pulled out the power lead and took it into the bedroom with me. I hid it in my underwear drawer and got back into bed.

~

I had spent a few hours scrolling on my phone for job advertisements, both in Oslo and Bergen, but there was very little, except for the odd cleaning job. I felt anxious that I didn't have the luxury to bide my time, as I had been forced to leave my current job rather than it being my decision.

I felt trapped in this little flat, in this little bedroom, but felt there was no option to go elsewhere. I had no work, of course, but all of my friends *were* at work. I pulled my baggage from Bergen out of my closet and nervously emptied the envelope of money under my duvet. 'Where can I hide it?', I thought. I looked around the room. I wandered into my bathroom and spotted a box of sanitary towels. I smiled to myself and brought a handful of them back to the bed I kept aside the rent due later that month and split the rest into 1,000 kroner bundles, hiding each batch in an empty towel package, and put them in the back of my underwear drawer with the power lead. I kept the rent money in the envelope and stored it in my cabin bag.

Around lunchtime, I wandered to the kitchen to find something to eat. The brothers were sitting on the sofa, playing games on their phones. I was so disappointed.

"Right," I said. "Let's talk."

The boys looked up at me.

"One second, let me just finish…"

I made myself a strong coffee and sat down at the breakfast bar, waiting for them, when I realised that they were still doing everything as before.

"Right, so now we talk," I interrupted their gaming.

Thor looked up at me with disdain, Kris didn't.

"So, I've decided to hand my notice in with the landlord," I started.

Thor smiled. "Fantastic! I'm glad you finally came round."

"No," I replied. "Not quite coming round, in that sense of the word."

"But now that we are all earning, we can afford one of the bigger places."

"Which brings me straight to that topic," I replied.

I decided in that moment to just focus on the financial side of things, and getting this place tidied up.

"So, I have calculated how much it costs to live here. The plan is to share all the costs three ways. Expenses bring us to 30,000 kroner a month right now. A bigger place would cost even more, so over the next couple of months we need to ensure that we can afford a bigger place. So, we need to bring in 10,000 kroner a month each."

Kristian looked up from his phone. "But I have to sleep on the sofa, I shouldn't have to..."

"I have to share a bed with Thor, and I also make meals for you, and had to clean up for you, which is also changing now."

"But he's your boyfriend, so you choose..."

"I don't care, if you don't like it, you can find your own place with your own bedroom. Now, back to the cleaning. This," I waved my arm around the room, "is getting cleaned up by you two, as you were the ones who made the mess. How are we meant to get a good reference from the landlord if he sees it in this state?"

"But he won't..." Kris started.

"Shut up, Kristian! Carpets NEED to be cleaned too, as it's not just surface mess like these cans and pizza boxes. There will be no smoking, EVER. Once this place is up to standard, then we can start cleaning up after us as we go along. If things don't go smoother, then we'll have to resort to cooking our own meals too. If this still doesn't work, then I'll be looking for my own place, and so will you."

"You earn more money than us though, so…"

I stopped him again, "That is your choice, if you don't earn enough to cover the expenses, then you need to find a better job, or a second job. It's not my concern, it's yours! Again, if you can't pay, you'll have to find somewhere else to live."

"I'm not doing it!" Kris' voice became louder.

"If you don't pay, you're out or your brother will pay your share." I looked at Thor. "If you can't afford it, then we won't be able to get a bigger place. If you don't want to clean up the mess, then get out, or again, your brother will have to do your share."

"What if we both refuse?"

"Then I'll be getting my own place. Simple as that."

"Well, it's shit living with you anyway!" Kris retaliated.

"Great. Get out then! Your parents came to see me in Bergen, I'm sure they'd happily take you back or help you get your own place. It's not my problem, it's yours!"

I felt proud of myself for being so strong, so I made myself another coffee and triumphantly returned to my bedroom.

Heidi Hansen

Chapter 11 – Oranges on Apple Trees

I had fallen asleep early the previous day, and didn't even wake when Thor came to bed. I looked at my phone, saw it was 10:15 and dragged myself out of bed. My tummy reminded me that I didn't eat yesterday. I padded into the kitchen for coffee, and noticed a slight improvement with the cleaning, but nowhere near decent. I assumed that they might be aiming for me to break and do it myself, but I had no intention. I searched for food while the coffee was brewing. The only food in the place was pasta and rice, and of course the meat cakes, salmon and soup in the freezer. I knew that wouldn't cut it, so I showered and dressed while drinking my coffee and headed out.

I didn't really fancy going to Marit's specifically, as it meant I'd have to walk past the office, but I knew I'd have to, sooner or later. I soon found myself outside the office after going into autopilot mode and habitually standing outside the door. It appeared that they were open again. I quickly walked away and headed towards Marit's coffee shop. As I approached I could see the queue, a sight I had been familiar with. I found myself feeling apprehensive and anxious as I waited. I could see all the tables were occupied, and decided that I should maybe find somewhere else. As I turned away, I heard someone say my name. I froze to the spot. A gentle hand rested on my shoulder; it was Erik, my ex.

"Line, how are you? I've been so worried about you! Come and sit with me." I nodded and nervously followed him in.

A few people looked up knowingly, whispering amongst themselves. I hesitated.

"Take no notice of them, they're just gossiping," Erik reassured me.

I sat down at the table where he had been drinking a coffee. I looked around and saw Marit, who briefly smiled at me before turning her attention back to her customer. I looked back at Erik. The shame I felt about how I treated him last Christmas resurfaced. I had chosen to kiss Thor and had let both Erik and myself down. And now he was sitting opposite me, smiling at me sympathetically.

"I'm sorry, Erik," I broke the silence, although it didn't feel awkward or uncomfortable.

"What for?" he asked.

"For the way that I treated you. It was unforgivable." Tears started welling in my eyes.

He leaned forward and passed me a napkin. "Hey," he whispered, "it's all water under the bridge now."

Marit appeared at our table, with a delicious-looking sandwich for Erik. "So good to see you, Line. It's seemed to have been ages."

"I'm so sorry, Marit," I replied, my stomach rumbling instinctively.

"She seems to be in an apologetic mood today," Erik laughed gently.

"Silly!" Marit exclaimed. "I'll try and come and talk to you shortly, if that's ok. Just got to clear the hordes a bit." She turned to Erik. "Did you want to order anything else, Erik?" she asked, pulling out her little order pad and a pen.

"I'm ok thanks," he replied, "but it sounds like my friend's stomach would?" He looked at me.

"Oh, I don't want to push into the queue," I replied. "I'll wait my turn."

"This is Erik's turn, and therefore your turn," Marit replied.

"Can I have a salmon sandwich, and a…"

"Hot chocolate?" Marit laughed.

I nodded. "Thanks, Marit."

"I'm not going to probe you for information about what happened last week," Erik explained. "But you can talk to me about anything you want to, and I'll be here for you."

I smiled, and felt more guilty. I wanted to rant about Thor, above all else, but knew this was a definite no-no topic.

"I got the sack," I blurted.

"Hansen sacked you because of what happened? That's low!"

"He's low," I laughed, "but no, he sacked me about 10 minutes before I found Aggie."

"Coincidence? Do you think he was… tying up loose ends?"

"Blimey, you should become a detective," I laughed, "that was quicker than my assumption!"

"I'm guessing you were in shock too much to even think about that?" Erik stated. I nodded. "How long is the notice period?"

"It was for a week, so, today I guess?"

"So, what's the next move for you?"

"I have no idea. I'm making some big changes in my life…" I didn't want to bring all that into the discussion. "I may even do a complete 360 and change careers altogether."

"I know how much you hated working there, so it sounds like a good move." He smiled, and I felt deceptive, and guilty again. "What do you fancy?"

"Huh?" I replied.

"Career?"

"Oh, I really don't know, to be honest, Erik," I smiled back at him; a nervous smile.

"Sorry for pushing," he replied.

"Now who's apologetic?!" I half-laughed.

Marit arrived with my order, and another coffee for Erik. "I thought you might need a top-up," she explained, sitting down at our table with another coffee.

"So how are you, Line?" she enquired.

"So-so," I replied, "my father whisked me away to Bergen for a few days," I explained.

"Ah, that's why I haven't seen you!" Marit exclaimed. "A few of the customers said that you must have been arrested."

"I'm a suspect?" I questioned.

"Only with the gossipmongers!"

I took in a big inhalation.

"Don't worry, Line, the important people know you wouldn't."

I sipped at my hot chocolate as I processed this new bit of information.

Erik seemed eager to change the topic. "Line got fired from her job there, Marit. She's thinking of switching her career up completely. What do you reckon she should try?"

"Well, I could do with an extra hand here. It probably wouldn't be a career for you, but certainly an inbetween job, if needed?"

"Oh, I don't think your customers would like that," I laughed. "Harbouring a killer!" I whispered surreptitiously.

"Well... as you can see, I rarely get a minute to myself. So maybe you could give it some thought? You'd be doing me a big favour. Even more so if you can bring in more nosey chinwaggers!" At that, she stood up and walked back to the counter.

As she passed by me, I saw Hansen enter the shop and I felt a wave of panic rising in me. "Shit!"

"It's ok, don't panic, I'm here with you."

I assumed that he'd get his stuff and go, or at worst stay at a table with a mysterious blonde, but no, he made a beeline for me.

"Sorry for your loss, Larsen." I was taken aback by this, and I thanked him. He leaned into me, "So will 'Larsen Detective Agency' be reporting to your boyfriend that you are having secret dates with your ex?" he probed sarcastically.

"It was just a coincidence," I replied, unnecessarily.

He strolled off confidently.

"You didn't need to justify yourself, you know?" Erik said.

I nodded. "I know, he just seems to be able to pull my strings."

"I know," he replied, smiling warmly. "I hate to say it, but I have to leave for work. It's been great to catch up with you. If you need anything, you have still got my number?"

I was visibly deflated. "No, I don't think so. Th… I was asked to delete it."

He pulled his wallet out of his pocket and sorted out some money for his food and drink. "Ok, I'll message you, and you can save my number under a different name, maybe? You still on the same number?

I nodded. "I'm sorry."

"Shush!" he replied. "I'll see you soon, hopefully."

I nodded and watched as he passed the money to Marit. A blonde lady passed by him as he left; it was Hanna. I noticed Hansen looking at me smugly, and shook his head. I took this opportunity to leave; he wouldn't be able to follow me, and his wife couldn't be around, he wouldn't allow that!

I got my purse out of my bag and approached the counter to pay. Marit shook her head.

"It's covered, paid for," she told me. I frowned. "Erik paid."

"He's so naughty! Can I put some money behind the counter to cover his next visit, please?"

"Or you could work here and do it then?" she smiled.

"You weren't joking?" I questioned and she shook her head. "It'd be a massive change to what I'm used to, though."

"Just what you need?" she suggested. "Tell you what – if you can get here for 5 a.m. tomorrow, I'll go through it with you. If you want to go ahead, then you can start there and then; if not, you're early enough to walk around the city looking for inspiration for jobs."

"WOW! Five?" I responded.

"Quite! Early, huh? I ideally need someone who could work from 6 a.m. until 2 p.m."

"I'm still on sedatives right now, but could just go to bed early," I smiled.

"Hopefully see you tomorrow then!" she replied, moving to serve a customer. "If you can't make it, or don't want it, then there's still no need to be a stranger."

I smiled and left her to it, trying my best to ignore Hansen as I left.

As I walked back to the flat, I found myself stopping outside the office again. There was a poster in the window, a reward for whoever killed Aggie. I felt a wave of nausea overwhelm me, and I steadied myself on the doorframe. It opened suddenly and I nearly fell to the floor.

"Hello, Miss Larsen," a voice said. It was Mr Olsen.

"Hello, Mr Olsen," I replied. "So you are back open?"

He nodded. "Yes. I would do anything to have Mrs Johnsen still here, she was a true marvel when it came to running the reception." He sighed. "I've been here today and luckily it's still quite quiet."

"Were all of the business owners cleared?"

"I believe so, yes. Some have now taken their business elsewhere, for their reputation and safety, though. Did you want to come in?"

I automatically clutched at my chest, struggling to breathe.

"Too soon?" he asked. I nodded.

"Not a problem. Feel free to pop in anytime."

"Thank you," I nodded and continued my walk back to the flat.

As soon as I arrived back, I could hear the brothers, before I saw them. I opened the door to the flat to find them playing games on the TV and console. They'd either found the power cord that I'd hidden, or they'd bought a new one.

"You're home early, Line," Thor announced, once he spotted me.

"And you've not done any cleaning or tidying up?" I responded.

Not even slightly, in fact! Nothing. Nada. Still disgusting. I aimed straight form my room, and my underwear drawer; firstly to see if that was where they had got the power lead from, but also, my secret stash of money. As I walked in, I saw my drawer almost on the floor, and what seemed like all of my little hidden wads of kroner. I squeezed them all individually as I returned them to my drawer – they seemed to be still ok, but I'd need somewhere better to hide them, or somewhere different to hide future items, like the power lead.

"Thought you could just hide the wire, eh?" Kristian said as he stood by my bedroom drawer.

I was livid. "This is NOT a game, Kris, you need to sort this shithole out!"

"Can't make me!" he replied smugly.

"I told you the rules this mor…"

"Who died and made you God?" he interrupted me. "It's not me who needs a regular shag!"

"Jesus Christ, Kris, what the hell, bro?" Thor stormed into the room. "Stop your arguing, both of you, or I'll knock your heads together!"

"WHAT??!" I screeched. "We are NOT children, this is your home for a maximum of two months. I've not yet written out the letter to the landlord, so I can always change that to one month! Then you can argue with him, not me!"

"Look, we're going to sort the flat out tomorrow while you are at work, so don't get your knickers in a twist!" He turned to Kris, "C'mon, bro, we need to go to work now."

I stayed in my room until they left, and then braved the living area. I couldn't keep living like this for two months, but was determined to leave all the mess for them to sort. I made myself a pot of coffee and sat at the breakfast bar, watching TV. It was all rubbish. Still full from my lunch, I decided to have a shower and a very early night. Whilst I was waiting for my meds to kick in, I thought more about Marit's job offer. Sure, it was nothing like what I was used to, or what my training was, but that was my plan anyway. Hopefully, I could get up early enough to get there at 5 a.m.

Heidi Hansen

Chapter 12 – Early Morning

I woke before my 4 a.m. alarm the next morning, raring to go. I felt a little strange, inside and out, but put it down to nerves. I got up and shuffled to my bedroom door. The light was still on in the living area, and I could see the devastation level had increased, so I retreated back to my room and into the bathroom. After a quick shower, I dressed and left.

It was a beautifully warm day, and I happily walked to Marit's coffee shop, arriving before she did. I sat on the floor outside and examined my phone. I had barely looked at it since yesterday afternoon. I had a text from Erik, stating that he was 'Erika', one from Pappa and two from Bella. I was tempted to reply, until I realised that it wasn't even 5 a.m.! I was sure that they wouldn't appreciate that.

The front door to Marit's unlocked and I stood up to greet her. She jumped back in mock surprise and I laughed. She let me in and then locked the door behind me. The coffee machine was already perculating, and Marit offered me a cup. We sat at a table together and sipped our coffee.

"Ok, down to business," Marit began. "Pros and cons of the job: Cons – it's early hours, as I mentioned yesterday, 6 a.m. until 2 p.m. I need someone who can help with the early mornings and the lunchtime rush, you see. As you have seen before, the queues are mental at times."

I nodded. This made me feel nervous. Although I much prefer being busy, work life with Hansen was very slow and I worried if I could cope.

"The next con is, obviously, the speed of the customers. However, this is something you will adapt to over time, and it shouldn't take too long to get used to."

"What if…" I started.

"I WILL give you all the training that you will need. There's usually two of us here at busy times, and adding you, or whoever joins the team, will make life much easier, not make more people stressed."

"Ok," I replied.

"This last one will probably be your biggest con. You may end up serving someone who you don't like, or who doesn't like you."

"Hansen?" I replied.

"Amongst others, yes. I had one of my girls whose ex kept coming in at very busy times."

"What did you do?"

"I banned him. I'd rather have happy staff than a problem customer. Now the pros. You get unlimited drinks. Maybe not constant hot chocolates with all the trimmings, but coffee and tea, and *some* cold drinks – especially when it's so warm like today. I like the staff to drink their drinks away from the customers, and there's a little staff area just through there." She indicated a door just by the side of the counter. "You get an hour's break for lunch. You don't get paid for the hour, but you can have a meal from here, to eat in the back or take out somewhere. Sometimes I ask for staff to have two half-hour breaks instead, especially when it is busy. Usually the break time is around 10, as that is when it gets a little quieter. It goes by so quickly that you rarely notice the time."

I nodded, "Just what I've always wanted, to be honest, I hate it when work isn't busy."

Marit smiled. "Ok. The job involves serving customers, making drinks, clearing tables, cleaning the equipment and the customer area. At first, you may not instinctively know when this should be done, and that is understandable. Again, you will be trained."

I nodded again. I really wanted to know what the wages were, but remembered that it was always a no-no to ask at an interview, and this appeared to be an interview! 'Always ask a question, but not about money, at the end of the interview to show you are keen and interested', Ingrid, my college tutor had said to all of us.

"Is there a dress code?" I asked.

"Sort of, yes. There's no uniform, I like freedom to express yourself. I ask staff to be mindful of what they are wearing. Noting too loose, as it could get caught up with machinery. Feet covered in case of scalding water spillage. Flat shoes just in case you suffer with footache from being on them all day – Oh, there is a stool just over at the other side of the counter, in case you need to sit. I prefer staff to be on the go all the time, there's nearly always something to do. Long hair must be tied back, and if you are handling food and drink then it's essential to wear a not-so-sexy hat." She chuckled to herself and pointed at her head.

"Oh, also, you said yesterday that you are taking sedatives?" she continued. I nodded. "Ok, it's none of my business, but as the business owner, I have to ensure that staff are not to handle machinery, or sharp or hot items if they are under the influence. So, while you remain on them, it'll mainly clearing tables and cleaning. I'll still train you on the counter stuff, so you can jump right into it when you are ready."

"As much as I think this is a great job…" I began.

"Oh, you don't want it?" Marit butted in.

"I was going to ask if it was worth it for you, if I can't do the full job?"

"Oh, yes! Very much so, in fact. If the interior is clean, it is more enticing for customers. Plus, health and safety guidelines insist on it, so I've been short-handed at times while my girls have been cleaning instead of serving." She stood up and walked to the counter. I wasn't sure if I should be following or not.

"Just realised that I'd written everything down, to make my life easier with interviews." She returned to her seat with a A4 notepad, and began adding ticks next to each bullet point. "Blimey!" she exclaimed, "nearly forgot about the pay."

I smiled and acted as if I hadn't thought of that either. "Ok, to start with it's a two-month trial. You don't have to stay as long as that if you don't like it, and obviously if there is a major issue, I can terminate too. Like if you beat up a customer or something." She laughed. "Ok, so for the first two months, it is 190 kroner an hour, then if you decide to stay, and I'm happy too, it goes up to 210 kroner an hour after the two month's review."

It was about the same that I earned from Hansen. I had mixed feelings about it but was happy to give it a try. "Oh, erm… I might need a day off for Aggie's funeral. Will that be a problem?"

"Oh, that's not a problem at all, Line. You get 28 days paid leave, and things like close friends or family funerals are extra too."

"Ok, well I like the sound of it. When do you want me to start?"

She looked at my head and then my feet. "Well, you have suitable clothing, comfortable shoes and I have spare hair ties, so now, if you can or want?"

"Deal!" I announced.

She led me into the staff area, where I could put my bag in a locker. I switched off my phone. "There's no phones or similar when you are working," she explained.

She showed me how to make sandwiches, which everyone reckons they can do, until they see how Marit does them! I was shown how to operate the coffee machine, and the till. There was a price list by the side of the till. Cleaning products were explained to me, and how thorough I had to be, especially since the pandemic. In no time, it was time to unlock the door, and I was asked to keep the door open, as it was such a warm day. A couple of fans were switched on, and I was told to sit on the counter stool to observe the staff at first.

I did as instructed, and marvelled at how well Marit and Frøya, the other assistant, worked together so smoothly. I doubted my abilities to do the same. Every so often, Marit would nod at me to clean a table. I found myself instinctively asking for cleaning equipment when it was required. When it was a little quieter, Frøya showed me where the dishwasher was, and the correct way to load it. I had stacked up the pots in the staff area until this point, which I was told was ok in the short term. During the 'slow' period, I made a mad dash to get the whole customer area cleaned, ready for the lunchtime rush. Frøya had her break during this time, and Marit insisted that I take a break when Frøya returned. I objected at first, seeing as I had spent most of the time on my special stool, but Marit explained that it was the law, so I sat and ate a sandwich.

In no time, it was time to leave. Marit took me to one side for a brief chat – I was worried that I had done something wrong.

"How was your first day?" she enquired.

"I absolutely loved it. The speed is daunting, but exciting, and I can't wait to keep up with you guys!"

"I bet you are tired now?" Marit asked.

I nodded. "Yes, I think I'll sleep well tonight!"

"Great!" Marit exclaimed. "Same again tomorrow? Except 6 a.m., of course."

"Most definitely," I responded.

"We'll sort out shifts tomorrow hopefully, although days could vary every week."

"Not a problem, Captain!" I saluted her, and she laughed.

I felt euphoric. The best I'd felt in a very long time. I wasn't ready to go home yet, and the Valles wouldn't be leaving for work for a couple of hours. My feet hurt from all of this activity, otherwise I would have had a trip around the shops, so instead I decided to bite the bullet and visit Mr Olsen.

He appeared to be delighted to see me, despite the fact that he was busy too. "I used to be able to do all this," he explained to me, "then Mrs Johnsen took the reins, and I *clearly* got too slack!"

"Oh, I only really worked with her for a couple of days, so can't shine any light on it either, sorry."

"Luckily, all the tenants are aware of the situation, so most are fairly understanding and patient," he continued. "I've not even had a break yet!"

"Oh, did you want me to man the desk for you for a bit?"

"Would you mind?" he asked.

"Not at all."

He almost leapt from his chair, patting it for me to replace him. "Are you sure?"

I nodded, sitting down, but ensuring that the chair faced away from the kitchen. Mr Olsen was only away for about 10 minutes, but it felt like days. I hated it.

"I'm so grateful for this, Miss Larsen, really I am," he beamed, as he returned to his seat with food from Marit's! "If there is any chance that you would consider... I know it is incredibly soon... if you would be interested in working here for me?"

I instinctively looked straight over to the kitchen and inhaled sharply. "Oh, Oh, I...I don't think I could, to be honest. I'm so sorry."

"It's not a problem, my dear," he replied.

"However, I have literally just started working at Marit's, today," I nodded to his food bag. "If you like, I can bring you some food round either on my break, or after I've finished?"

"Oh, that's a very kind offer. I'm so disorganised these days, that I don't get a chance to prepare myself anything."

"Not a problem, just let me know what you want and if you want it at around 10 a.m., or 2 p.m., although my days or times could change, apparently. But we can do it day by day?"

"Yes, that would be amazing. Could I do both times, please? I also struggle to go into the kitchen. I think I'm going to get it refitted and spruced up a bit."

"Excellent. Happy to help. If I bring you a drink during my break time, and then you tell me what you want for after I finish?" I suggested.

"I don't want to disturb your break time though?"

"It's not an issue, It's only a few minutes away."

"That sounds great then," he agreed.

He told me how he wanted his coffee, and that a pastry would be nice too, 'it will probably be a slippery slope downhill though!', he'd said.

We sat and chatted, mostly about Aggie, until we both realised the time. I left him to do the closing chores and headed back to the flat. I stopped at a nearby park, and sat on a bench. I was biding my time until the brothers would leave for work, and busied myself with the task of replying to phone messages. I was incredibly tired, after such a long day. I checked the time and figured it would be safe to complete my journey now.

I was correct, the boys had left the flat for work. It was fairly tidy, but nowhere need up to spec. I shrugged, and went straight to my bedroom, falling asleep almost immediately after taking my medication and checking my money stash.

Chapter 13 - And You Tell Me...

I felt Thor climb into bed just moments after I had become conscious that morning. I lay quiet, waiting for him to fall asleep, and then a little longer - just to be sure. I rolled over to grab my phone from the bedside drawer and checked the time - 04:30. Perfect! My alarm was set for just a half an hour later. I cancelled the alarm, and gently rolled out of bed. I tiptoed towards the doorway, to check if Kristian was asleep too. I could hear him snoring! I wasn't sure how I could proceed now, as I wanted a shower and a coffee before work, but didn't want to wake either of my flatmates. I was the only heavy sleeper, and that was because of my meds. I must admit - I did like the better sleep I got, and hoped I wouldn't become addicted.

I opened my phone to check for messages, and found one each from Bella, Pappa and Catrine, congratulating me for getting two job offers so quickly after being sacked. I decided to set a reminder to reply to them on my break.

I browsed the internet for a bit, looking for something along the lines of mixed martial arts and self-defence so that I could catch up with the others, but after work if possible. I found the place where the classes were held, and found that the place was a gym that was open 24 hours, seven days a week. They didn't sign new people up outside of their office hours, but I filled in an online form to go for a visit after work - well, after I had delivered Mr Olsen his food. It didn't solve my shower and coffee dilemma this morning, but could be an option before and after work to avoid being around the boys, and the flat that I no longer loved.

I bit the bullet and ventured into the kitchen to make a coffee and then took it back into the bedroom. I sat back in my chair and browsed the internet a little longer as I sipped my hot beverage. I checked the time regularly so that I wasn't late for work. I didn't want to risk having a shower and waking Thor up, but I also hated the thought of *not* having a shower before work, especially at the height of summer. I sprayed extra deodorant and perfume on, not enough to overwhelm others though, and dressed in lightweight clothes suitable for work *and* the gym.

Work was great, nice and busy. I explained my plan to take Mr Olsen food and drink, explaining that he couldn't get out of the building. She said it was fine, and I continued with the plan of taking him a large coffee during my break, and taking my lunch with me.

I sat with him and chatted for a while, and even chatted with Nora when she brought his mail. I knew I would always struggle being so close to the murder scene, and Mr Olsen, or Einar, as he insisted I call him, ensured that I sat at the other end of reception, but not in the eyeline of the kitchen.

I told Einar about my gym booking for that afternoon. He tried to ask me to not worry about delivering his lunch, but I assured him that the booking was not until 15:30, so he had no reason to worry. He seemed to be happier with that, and chose a sandwich from the menu I had brought him, along with another coffee, and he gave me some money to cover it. When I returned after work, I gave him his food and sat with a coffee and chatted again, and then headed for the gym.

My feet still ached from the day's work, but managed to walk around the gym as the personal trainer showed me around. I was allowed a free session after that, and chose to stay off my feet as much as possible – things like treadmills could wait until my days off! Satisfied that I had done well on the rowing machine and weights, so had a shower and then a coffee. Foolishly, I had forgotten clean clothes, but made a mental note to remember next time. I found that I could store my clothes in a locker, if I could get myself a padlock for it. I'd look for one on the way home.

~

When I finally got back to the flat, I was faced with quite a surprise; the flat was almost spotless! I closed the door warily, and walked slowly around the whole place. In the kitchen, I found an envelope with my name on it. I opened it. Inside was some money and a letter. I chose to read the letter first.

Hi Line

We seem to keep missing each other, guess those sedatives are messing with your sleeping pattern?

We've cleaned the place up, like you wanted, and have hired an upholstery cleaner so that we can clean the sofa and carpet tomorrow.

The money in the envelope is the 5,000 kroner weekly payment, if it is ok to pay weekly?

See you tonight, or possibly when you wake in the morning. I don't mind being woken up.

Love you lots

Thor

xxxxxxxxxx

I pulled the money out of the envelope and yes, it was 5,000 kroner. I felt totally guilty now! I put the money back into the envelope and placed it in the food cupboard for safekeeping. My first thought then was to make them a nice supper for when they got home. My second thought, more cynical, was to check my underwear drawer and closet to make sure the secret money was all still there. Surprisingly, it was. I decided that I needed a better place to hide it though.

I returned to the kitchen to see what I could make for their supper. All that there was in the cupboard was still only rice and pasta. They hadn't had either for a while. I was too exhausted to go to the local grocery shop to get extra ingredients. I remembered that there was salmon in the freezer, that Pappa had given me. I found the tub and looked inside. Five pieces, excellent! He had also told me that rice shouldn't be kept at certain temperatures as it can get bacteria in it, or something like that, so I emptied the bag of pasta into a saucepan and cooked it. I wouldn't need to cook their salmon as they could do it when they were reheating their pasta, so I just put one on each plate, knowing that they'd defrost in time for supper. I wrote a quick note while it was cooking, apologising that I'd been sleeping so long, and that I would go grocery shopping over the weekend to get more meals. I prepped the ingredients for the breadmaker and set a timer for tomorrow morning. I chose to have my dinner now, so I could have an early night, and within 20 minutes, it was ready. I dished the pasta between three of us, and put their plates in the microwave. I sat at the breakfast bar to eat, and watched some TV, before having a shower and going to bed.

Chapter 14 – You Wanted More

Again, I woke as Thor was getting into bed, and waited for him to fall asleep. My plan was to go to the gym, have coffee, and then have some time on the rowing machine before work. I also planned to store my surplus money in the gym locker, as I figured it'd be safer there than at home with the boys. I planned what clothing I'd need to take with me; spare clothes for work, and clean gym clothing for this evening, which was self-defence class with the girls. I'd also need going out clothes for afterwards. And a towel! The gym has lent me one yesterday, but that was a one-off.

Once I was sure that Thor was asleep, I grabbed a drawstring bag and started loading the belongings into it. I added the towel, the money and a padlock that I'd found in the bathroom cupboard. I'd signed up to a membership at the gym yesterday and ensured that my member ID card was in my little rucksack, alongside my purse and flat keys.

I tiptoed into the kitchen, my nose navigating me to the bread machine which had baked a loaf overnight, and I put it on the breadboard and cut myself a slice. I placed all of the jars of spreads next to it, so that the boys would see it. I realised that their plates were not in the sink, and was pleased until I found them still in the microwave, and then discovered empty pizza boxes in the bin. 'At least they're in the bin, I guess', I thought. I spread my slice of bread with butter and left for the gym, spotting a hairbrush on my way out of the flat.

It was still a little dark outside, and I worried about potential threats, especially with so much money in the gym bag. I chose to not listen to music on the way, to stay aware of my surroundings.

Arriving safely, I stored everything, got changed and headed to the rowing machine. I kept my phone with me, and plugged the earphones in to listen to my music. I had an alarm set on my phone to let me know when it was time for work, and this sounded after about 45 minutes. I showered and changed and grabbed a coffee before leaving for work.

In the staff room, I spotted the new timetable, which had been displayed on the wall. It appeared that I would only need to be in on weekdays, following the same shifts that I was now used to.

"I have a girl who is at college, and she can only work at weekends," Marit said from behind me.

"Looks good to me," I replied, smiling.

The day went quickly, as did the trips to Mr Olsen, Einar, with his coffee and lunch orders. I sat with Einar after work, with a plan to head back to the gym for a shower and change ready for the self-defence class. I studied him as he worked, his salt and pepper hair perfectly neat and tidy, and his clothes showing the level of class, and possibly wealth that he had. He looked totally professional and started to get more comfortable in his new role. There was a job vacancy poster for this receptionist job stuck to the window, as it became clear that he felt out of his depth covering for Aggie.

A man came by, looking grey and haggered with grief, who wasn't one of the tenants of the building, and introduced himself. It was Mr Johnsen, Aggie's husband. I gasped and stood up, next to him in seconds to greet him.

"I'm so, so terribly sorry for your loss," Einar spoke with sincerity. "She was a huge asset to the team and will be sorely missed." He gestured to me. "This is Miss Larsen, Line, she was…"

"I know who she is, thank you Mr Olsen." He turned to face me. "Miss Larsen, Aggie thought the world of you. I am so grateful for the time you spent with her, making her work life even better, and for staying with her till the end. I'm sure you miss her as much as I do."

I felt tears welling in my eyes. "She was such a great lady, and a genuine friend to me," I replied, shaking his hand.

"The coroner has finally released her... her body, and the funeral is booked. It would be lovely for you both to come, if you can?"

We both nodded. He thanked us again and left the building.

We both stood in silence for a few minutes. "He looks much older than he used to," Einar explained. "It must have taken its toll on him. I wonder how her sons are, too."

I nodded. "I've never met him, nor really heard much about him except that they were solid, and happy."

I left as Einar closed up the building, and he waved goodbye as he walked to the car park. I stood for a second, and noticed a small bunch of flowers laying on the floor by the door. I crouched down to examine them and found a card. It simply read 'GONE TOO SOON.' I remained silent for a moment and then placed the flowers where I had found them.

I stood up again, ready for my walk to the gym.

"You're going the wrong way!" I turned round to find Thor standing at the corner of the building.

"What are you doing here?" I asked, surprised to see him.

"We need food, so figured I'd come to the store with you."

I had planned to go tomorrow or Sunday, depending on the work pattern of the two brothers. "Oh, I was going to go sometime over the weekend. I figured that you would be on your way to work today?"

"Naa, I get Fridays off. I will be working all day tomorrow though, so you can chill all day then."

"I don't have any of the money on me."

"That's ok," he replied. "I have some on me, we can use that and then I can replace it with the money we left for you."

There was no way out of doing this, so I nodded and we made our way there.

I was grateful that Kristian wasn't with us, because he was like a child in a sweet shop when in stores, wanting everything he sees. It was bad enough with Thor, who was placing really expensive foods into the trolley. I usually opted for cheap pasta and rice, but he was choosing brand-named products. He was also picking up desserts, and snacks. I couldn't really argue with him, as we were now getting three people to pay for the household expenses. By the end of the trip, we had spent three times as much as usual on groceries. As we stepped outside, Kristian appeared, ready to help carry the shopping home.

We all helped to put the products in their correct place. I looked at the time on my phone and saw that I was too late for the girl's night. Thor insisted that I sit on the freshly cleaned sofa and pulled out a couple of DVDs that he had bought, that we could apparently watch tonight. They weren't films that I would enjoy, but I did use to badger him into watching TV with me, so I couldn't really complain. He took my shoes off my feet, which made me feel a bit weird, and told me to relax while he cooked us a late dinner. Kristian went out for the night with a couple of friends from work, so it was a romantic evening for two.

He brought me a large glass of wine, and chatted to me while he was cooking. I disappeared briefly for a quick shower and changed into my pyjamas, returning just in time for when Thor was plating up the meal. It looked like a massive feast, with slices of meat, cubes of potatoes which were soft and crispy, a variety of vegetables and a gravy.

"It's a traditional roast dinner, like they make in England," he responded to my puzzled expression. "I remember you were learning the language." I nodded, smiling. "Well, here we have chicken. Which they call 'kylling', potatoes, or 'poteter', with peas, 'erter' and your favourite, 'kål'," he pointed to the cabbage.

We sat on the sofa together to eat our dinner while watching TV, which wasn't easy with the gravy. "Jeg elsker kål," I said to him, which means 'I love cabbage'.

"Jeg elsker du," he replied, kissing me.

He took the plates into the kitchen, and I could hear him clattering about.

"Et voila!"

"That's French, isn't it?" I queried.

He laughed. "Yeah, but this dessert is definitely English. It's called 'brød og smør pudding', which is bread and butter pudding."

It was delicious. I looked forward to being able to go to England one day.

Once we had finished, Thor took the pots into the kitchen and washed up everything.

~

"Line, wake up!" Thor shouted at me. I opened my eyes as best as I could, and he was sitting on the sofa, glaring at me.

"Huh?" was all that I could manage.

"It's meant to be a date night!"

"Huh?" I repeated.

"WHY ARE YOU SLEEPING?? WE ARE MEANT TO BE HAVING A ROMANTIC EVENING. I MADE US FOOD!"

"I can't help it if I can't stay awake…" I tried explaining.

"YES, YOU CAN!" he replied.

I stood up. "I'm going to bed."

"WHAT?? ARE YOU SERIOUS??"

"Yeah, I'm tired."

Chapter 15 – Touchy

When I awoke the next day, I felt sore. Clearly I had overdone it at the gym this week. I decided that today should be a nice relaxing day. I rolled over to get my phone from the bedside table, but it wasn't there. I frowned, and got out of bed to search for it underneath. Nothing! I ventured into the living area and found it on the breakfast bar. This wasn't like me, but I had gone to bed after I had nodded off, so probably didn't think about taking it with me.

It was nice and quiet in the flat, with both boys at work. The pots from last night's meal were still on the counter, so I quickly washed them up while I waited for the coffee to brew. I felt grubby from, looking at the state of my bedcovers, a rough night's sleep, so I took my coffee, and the pot back into my room and changed the bedcovers on my bed before having a shower. I felt so much better after that and settled into my bed again. I discovered a couple of streaming channels with apps that I could download on my phone, so I relaxed watching trashy TV for most of the morning.

Around the time I finished the coffee, I found that I was still in pain so I got up and looked around for some painkillers. I figured that my period was due, I had never really monitored it before, which must be the cause for the pain, which was mainly internal and also around my hips. I had possibly pushed it on the rowing machine, which I made a mental note to switch up with other equipment when I returned. All in all, though, I had thoroughly enjoyed it and was pleased that I had become a member.

As Thor had used the rest of the loaf of bread for last night's dessert, I filled up the bread machine with the necessary ingredients and set the timer for tomorrow morning. I looked in the food cupboard and was amazed at how much we had bought yesterday. I spotted some muesli, which I poured into a bowl, and some yogurt in the fridge, which I poured on top. I returned to my bed with the coffee pot and my late breakfast.

I wasn't sure what time Thor would be home, and didn't want to text him after his outburst last night. I feared that his mood could be the same today, so felt a little apprehensive. I picked up my phone to check my messages and found a couple. Erik, code name 'Erika' had messaged me to see how the first week of my job had gone. I replied now, even though I knew he would be at work today, as Saturdays were their most busy.

'Hey. First week went well, thanks for asking. So glad I took the plunge and switched it up! Hope you are good?'.

I continued to scroll and found one from Belle. She was asking if I'd be going to the girl's night out last night.

'Hey. So sorry, Tinkerbell. Thor met me after work and took me shopping. I WILL be there next week though! L xx'.

She replied almost immediately.

"Hey, you. No worries about last night, although it was a blast so it would have been a good one for you. Take care. B xx'.

I was sad that I had missed a good night out, it had been weeks since I had attended. Before Aggie's murder, I hadn't been able to go due to having little money, but now that the boys were paying their way, it would be a little better in future. I wanted to probe Bella a bit more about what they did, but the 'take care' made me think it was a closed response. Or maybe I was just still a little paranoid since last night's argument with Thor. I knew that being dosed up with these sedatives didn't help, well they didn't help my relationship with Thor, but they definitely assured that I wouldn't have any more restless nights. I made a note on my phone to contact the doctor about the meds next week.

I got up and returned to the kitchen, mainly for more food but also a different drink. I opted for some of the wine from last night, and for food I discovered some ready-to-eat mashed potato, which I paired with Pappa's meat cakes out of the freezer.

I was just devouring my second ice cream when the brothers came home, quite inebriated. I checked the time on my phone, it was 23:00.

"Ahh there she is, look," Thor yelled. "She can't stay awake for a little romance, but can be up this late to reprimand me for drinking after work!"

"I wasn't going to..." I started.

"No, you never are, are you?!" he interrupted.

"I've slept for some of the day, that's w..."

"Cut the crap, Line," he continued to berate. "Well, we," he indicated himself and his brother, "are going to be doing some more gaming, so you can fuck off back to the bedroom!"

I stood up dutifully, carrying my wine and what was left of my ice cream, and went to my room.

I lay awake for hours, wondering how long they would be up for. Realising that the noise level was not going to simmer down just yet, I took two sedatives. It was so warm that I decided to open the curtains to let some more air into the room. I saw a quick flash in the night sky; it looked like I was in for a stormy night, both figuratively and literally. Fortunately, or unfortunately, depending on the point of view, I fell asleep quite quickly.

Chapter 16 – Dragonfly

I again woke to an extremely quiet flat. I wasn't sure if the boys were at work or just out. I looked at the time on my phone and found that it was 13:11; I'd slept for over 12 hours! I'd wasted valuable time, and swore to myself that not only will I not mix the sedatives with wine in future, but also I would not double the dose!

I got up, showered and entered the kitchen for coffee. This also prompted me to not try and balance my sleeping pattern with coffee either. 'Maybe I should get some decaf coffee!', I thought to myself. I checked the bread machine and the loaf it had produced looked magnificent. I carved a few slices, and then wrapped the rest up in a beeswax wrap, placing it into the bread tin. I left the door open a bit so that the boys would be alerted to something being in there. Although I had just pledged to cut down the caffeine levels, I felt like I needed a pick me up, so chose honey to spread on my bread. 'This meal could be 'brunch', I decided, cutting a couple more slices. I took my plate over to the sofa, but it smelled of feet and something else I didn't want to smell, so returned to my bedroom. I sat in the chair so that I wouldn't get crumbs on the sheets.

I realised how much more I was eating when home alone, and decided it was due to boredom. I needed something to keep me occupied at weekends – that or a second job! I chose to switch to only water once I had been for a shower, and dressed for a hike. I hadn't been able to get far the last time, but at least I had been with family. Now that I was going to go on my own, it was a little more of a worry. It had been my sedatives that had knocked me off my feet before. I guessed I should just be more careful.

I packed an energy bar into my little rucksack bag, and put my water bottle in there too. I put my earphones in, with the phone in my shorts pocket and I set off. It was a beautiful day, and I felt the sun's rays warming my skin. Despite my music blaring in my ears, I kept an eye on my surroundings; nothing wrong with super-vigilance! I headed to Marit's first, hoping for one of her delicious slushies. There wasn't much of a queue, luckily, and I was served in no time.

"What are you doing here on a Sunday?" Marit laughed. "Will I have to start paying you to get you out?"

I laughed. "I'm just getting a little stir-crazy right now. Had to get out and do something so thought I'd have a little hike."

"Well don't overdo it, I still need you here tomorrow morning, six SHARP!" She smiled at me.

It was nothing compared to one of Aggie's funny faces, but it was nice to have a friendly face to work with. I didn't miss working with Hansen at all!

"I will be there!" I pledged.

I left the shop with a smile on my face, which became broader when I bumped into Erik in the queue.

"Hey," he greeted me.

"Hey, Erik," I responded, "what are you up to today?"

"Day off," he replied, "so absolutely nothing. You?"

"Just going for a hike or walk."

"Well, don't overdo it!"

"I won't," I replied, smiling, and went on my way.

I walked at a gentle pace and arrived at a park with a small body of water. Lots of children were running around and splashing in the water. Parents were sitting on blankets or folding chairs, eating lunch. One family had brought a swing ball set. Another had frisbees. There were also a few balls shooting around.

I sat underneath a tree, smiling at the happy children. Out of the corner of my eye I spotted Heidi. 'Why is she even here? She doesn't even have children!' I thought, before realising that neither do I! She made a beeline for me. And I held my breath. Surely she wouldn't make a scene here?

"Hello, Line," she began, kneeling down next to me. "How are you, following ... what happened to your friend?"

"It's been hard," I replied, scared of how close she was to me.

"Have they found who did it?" she enquired.

I looked at her through squinted eyes. How dare she talk to me about this.

"No," I shook my head. "They've questioned you though, haven't they?"

She nodded. "Yes, because I attacked her last year, I was a suspect for a short time. Apparently I was also in the building at the time she was murdered."

She was so flippant with her storytelling, and her attempts at innocence! I wanted to open up to her, but knew that it wasn't a viable option, especially as I was convinced that she was the murderer! There wasn't really anyone who I could talk to about it.

Hansen suddenly appeared, telling Heidi to get up. He looked odd, wearing beige combat shorts and a blue t-shirt. The shirt brought out the vivid blue of his eyes, which I'd normally be attracted to, but not when it was that slimeball. He had a professional-looking camera on a strap around his neck.

"Are you a keen photographer, Mr Hansen?" I enquired sarcastically.

"I have been known to dabble."

I looked around. All that was here was happy families and small children. I shuddered at the thought of him taking photos of the young and innocent.

"Have your own darkroom in your basement?" I cringed.

"I do actually. The wildlife can be fascinating in such a highly populated city. It is normally assumed that it is more diverse in the forests and coast, but there are some amazing creatures… Insects, like that dragonfly over there by the water…" I didn't like the idea of him even looking by the water where all the kids were playing. "There are such beautiful birds…" I lost interest at this point, assuming that he was referring to 'birds' as being a slang term for women. "Come on then, wife, let's leave the poor girl alone!" he grabbed her hand tightly at the wrist and guided her away.

'Let's hope she kills him next!', I thought to myself.

I sat and watched the dragonfly bobbing around the water, the beautiful colours of the wings playing tricks on us all..

I put my sunglasses on and lay down. I started to think about what to have for dinner, and realised that food was beginning to take over my mind and my life when I wasn't working. I would certainly need to get to the gym more, before I started to put on weight! My stomach rumbled so I decided to head home.

I plugged in my earphones and set off. Just before I turned into my street, I noticed a car similar to Hansen's parked nearby. As I got nearer, I saw that it *was* him! I switched my phone to the camera setting and discreetly took some photos, pretending I was on a facetime chat. My eyes were shielded by my sunglasses, so he couldn't see where I was actually looking.

"Who you talkin' to?" Kristian suddenly appeared, seemingly from nowhere. Thor was close behind.

"Oh, erm… I'll tell you in a couple of minutes."

"No!" Thor raised his voice. "WHO are you talking to?!"

I shut the camera app and put my phone in my pocket. "I'll explain when we get home," I insisted.

He snatched the phone from my pocket. "What's the password?"

"THORFINN <3," I replied.

He paused for a moment, probably touched that I had his name for it.

When we got back, I asked for my phone back.

"Who is Erika?" he asked.

'Think, Line, think!'. "I met Erika at the coffee shop recently, and she started to teach me a little English."

"Just from a random stranger??"

"Yeah, well, friend of Marit, who owns the shop."

"What did you learn?" he put me on the spot.

"Kaffe is coffee, melk is milk, smørbrød is sandwich. I'm probably getting the pronunciation completely wrong!" I laughed nervously. "I'm certainly a slow learner!"

"Not bad," he commented, passing the phone back.

"What's for dinner?" Kris piped up.

"I'm not sure yet," I replied. "Fancy anything in particular? Take a look at all the stuff that Thor got for us!"

He bounded into the kitchen and banged around for a bit. "There isn't anything!" he announced. "Shall we order a takeaway?"

"No," Thor and I replied simultaneously. We both laughed.

"I'm going for a quick shower, can you look for something please?"

"Why do I have to do that as well?" he complained.

"As well as…?" I challenged him. "You chose what to buy this week, so you must have had some meal ideas?" I left him to it and went into my room, plugged my phone into its charger and had a shower.

I returned after my shower to find the ingredients for hot dog waffles. 'Ugh!' I thought to myself. I really was sick of them. Nevertheless, I cooked the meal and the boys loved them. The salmon were still in the microwave, and I knew they wouldn't be any good now, which disappointed me. I threw them in the bin.

"We have some princess pudding for dessert," Thor announced.

I was rarely a dessert kind of girl, but with me not enjoying my dinner, I passed it on to Kristian – the human dustbin – and returned to the kitchen to serve the sweet course. It was delicious! I really needed to go to the gym daily to keep an eye on my weight!

Heidi Hansen

<u>Chapter 17 – I Won't Forget Her</u>

I went to bed fairly early the previous night, ready for work today. Neither of the Valles were aware of my new job, and that was fine by me, as I could imagine that Kris, especially, would be in constantly, to play up like a child, or ask for free food and drink. Truth be known, I'd rather deal with the Hansens.

I'd given Thor time to get into a deep sleep before quietly dressing, before leaving for the gym. Coffee. Get changed. Gym (rowing machine, weights, exercise bike). Shower. Get changed. Coffee. Work. Coffee. Coffee to Einar Olsen during my lunch break. Coffee. Coffee (repeat as necessary). Take lunch to Einar. Coffee. Go to gym. Coffee. Get changed. Gym. Shower. Get changed. Coffee. Home. Eat. Shower. Bed. This routine became the norm for my weekdays, dodging sleeping patterns for the most.

There was a break in the routine about a week or so in; I'd lost track of time, to be honest! It was Wednesday, and I had a day off as it was Aggie's funeral. I don't like funerals – then again, not many do, I guess. Today I had to creep around and hope to not wake either of my flatmates up. Thor was snoring his head off and Kristian appeared to be out since last night (unless he had suddenly decided to fold his covers up when he went out). I dressed simply in black loose trousers and a sleeveless black top – it was the height of summer and I didn't want to worry about being too hot.

I had booked a cab for 10:30 and planned to leave the flat just before, so that the taxi didn't use his horn and wake Thor up. I crept around, although Kris' absence made life easier, as I could have a coffee. I drank one cup and then filled a travel cup full too, which fitted nicely in the black bag I was taking with me. I didn't want to drink too much in case there weren't any bathroom facilities. I left a couple of minutes before the cab, quietly locking the door and tiptoeing downstairs, to the car park outside. I was surprised to find a visitor there as I exited. Erik!

"What are you doing here?" I questioned him, while looking up at the flat window to make sure that no one was awake.

"I figured you could do with having someone with you today," he replied. "Funerals aren't easy at the best of times," he continued, "unless you have someone going with you already?"

I looked up at the window again, as the taxi arrived. "Thanks, Erik, that would be great!"

I smiled weakly and we both got into the car. We sat quietly during the short journey across the city. As we arrived, so did Aggie's coffin. I felt sick already, wishing I'd either eaten something, or not had the coffee, I wasn't sure. I decided it was just part of the grief. I asked the taxi driver to park a little way from the entrance, to allow the family and friends go in before we did. We sat quietly at the back of the church. I would not cry, I had decided, as that is for the family and friends. I did feel emotional though, as visions of the scene kept flooding back to me.

We all moved to the graveside; I chose again to stand back. It became quite dark, clouds replacing the previously sunny day. There was a flash, and I couldn't help but think that Aggie had summoned it herself, to make her departure a dramatic one. I hadn't brought anything to cover me, which was stupid of me. I crossed my arms and held my hands under them for warmth. Erik instinctively put his arm around me, and there was another flash, which made me jump. Luckily there was no thunder. I could never remember whether it was the time difference between the thunder and lightning, or from lightning to thunder anyway, but that wasn't going to happen so it must have been far away. I looked around at all of the other cemetery plots, and spotted someone standing by a nearby tree. I squinted my eye to try and block out the surrounding area and saw that it was Heidi! THE NERVE! I strode right over there, Erik trying to keep up with me. He touched my shoulder when I was almost there, and whispered in my ear.

"Wait till the family have gone, Line."

"How dare you be here, Heidi," I whispered angrily. "You MURDERED her!" I was gritting my teeth. "You took my friend away from me, you stole her from her family," I gestured toward the remaining family at the graveside.

"I'd known Agnes for years, a long time - even before you arrived. I swear I didn't kill her, Line. I think it was Kenneth, and I think I'm next."

This took me aback. "No, Heidi, don't shift the blame. He's a snake, admittedly, but it was you who came out of the building last. Washing your hands, the blood off your hands."

"And who was second out? Who had time to murder someone while waiting for me?"

"NO. YOU BEAT HER NOT THAT LONG AGO!" I had completely lost my temper by this point. "YOU THREATENED HER. YOU SAID YOU WOULD KILL HER…"

"It's him, Line, it's him! And it could be you after me! For investigating for me, for crossing him! We need to get him before he gets us!" she was still shouting as I was guided away by Erik.

"Did you want to go to the grave site to say goodbye?"

I shook my head. I should have protected her, I said my goodbyes as I had held her in my arms, with blood dripping between my fingers. I was the last person that she saw before she was taken away from us, except, maybe, the murderer. I had no right to be emotional.

It looked like none of her family heard me shouting, I should have had more restraint. Mr Olsen approached me. I hoped that he hadn't heard me either, shouting like a fishwife, as my mother would say.

"Hello, Line," he started, "how are you doing?!

"It's hard, I feel so bad for her family. I should have done more, should have been there…"

"No, that's not your fault, it's whoever did this!" I nodded, he squeezed my hand. "I have closed the office today, as a mark of respect. Would be good to see you tomorrow."

I nodded again. He walked over to speak to the family. I felt too much shame to go to them.

"Can we go now, please?" I pleaded with Erik.

He nodded and ordered a taxi.

~

Back at the flat, Erik asked if I wanted him to come in with me.

"Can I check… if erm… anyone is in?" I replied, not wanting to mention Thor and his brother.

I quickly dashed upstairs and found no one else there. I shut the bathroom door that led to the bedroom and then the door to my bedroom. I beckoned to Erik and he came upstairs. He insisted on making me a coffee so I sat down on the tidy sofa.

"You got rid of your favourite chair?" he enquired.

"No, it's in the bedroom," I replied, not wanting to elaborate.

He brought me the coffee and sat down next to me.

"I'm sorry about the shouting. I hope it didn't embarrassment you?"

"I was a little disappointed..." he replied, "I thought you would shout a little more!" He smiled at me.

"What was she doing there, anyway?" I mused.

"Killers like to either visit the scene of the murder site or take part in searches, so maybe it's that sort of mentality?" he replied.

"It's not just me, is it?" I asked. "That thinks it was her, I mean."

"You said that Heidi was the last one in the building?"

I played it out in my head again. "I got to the main door of the building and Hansen was holding it open," I explained, with my eyes shut to picture it better. "Heidi came out of the bathroom and came to the door."

"And she said she suspected her husband?"

"Yeah."

"Could it have been possible, in your opinion?"

I thought for a second. "There was a lot of blood, but no footprints. I got blood on me when I tried to help her, but would the killer have blood on them from stabbing her?"

"Where was the blood?" he probed.

"It was on the floor."

"Any on her front?"

"I don't know," I replied, frustrated with myself.

"OK, don't stress about it. I assume the knife, or sharp object wasn't recovered?"

"No it wasn't."

"Well that rules out accident, or suicide, which is what the police probably decided because of the lack of weapon. So the killer took it away with them, right?"

"They could have disposed of it somewhere, thrown it out of the car or something?"

"Hmmm… yes, but… did either of them have anywhere to hide it? A bag, briefcase, big pockets?"

"Ohhh, of course… I see where you're going there." I racked my brains for a few moments. "Hansen had his briefcase. I think Heidi had a bag too."

"We need to know if the police found any blood drops to, or in, the ladies' bathroom."

"Or the men's?" I replied.

"Or a trail from the kitchen to the main door. Or at the door, when Hansen was standing there waiting?" Erik suggested, his steely-blue eyes pulling me in.

"*Or* the kitchen sink?"

He nodded. "We need to find out!" he concluded.

Realising how warm the flat was, I stood up to open the curtains, now back on their rail, and opened the windows. I saw a flash of lightning outside and mentioned it to Erik. He joined me at the window.

"The sky is blue, Line, there's no lightning."

Just then, there was another flash. "That's not lightning, Line. It's like a camera flash." He leaned out the window more. "It wasn't from the ground, as you saw it above you, right?" I was very aware of Erik being so close to me that he could touch me. I felt goosebumps all over my skin.

"Yeah, it was like over there," I pointed to the building opposite.

"Do you know anyone who lives or works over that way?"

I shrugged and shook my head. "Do you think someone is taking photos of *me*?"

"Do you only see the flashes when you are by the window?"

I thought for a second. "I don't know. I don't know whether they were actually lightning or just flashes."

"Ok, just keep an eye on it now. Think of the main tips: don't be naked near the window, don't undress near the window; stuff like that." He blushed a little.

"Ok, I will."

"I have to go now," he said. "I couldn't get the night off work."

"Oh, ok, thank you so much for coming with me."

We had an awkward moment of whether we should hug, shake hands or high five, opting for a slow saunter to the door and a random wave. I watched him descend the stairs and he waved again. I had another guilty feeling, I should never have let him go. Well, discard, mistreat, cheat.

I was driving myself mad, so I went for a shower and climbed into bed.

Chapter 18- The Blue Sky

I must have been exhausted from the funeral, as I didn't wake until my alarm. I had missed out on the gym opportunity, but knew I'd be there after work, once I'd sorted Einar's lunch.

I arrived at work right on time, which was the latest I'd ever got there. Marit hugged me and asked me about the funeral.

"I kinda had a row with Heidi," I told her.

"WOW! At the funeral?"

"Yeah, the nerve of her, going to the funeral!"

"It is rather strange. What did you say to her?"

"I told her that she had no right to be there. That I was certain that she murdered her. But here's the even stranger thing; she reckons that Hansen killed Aggie and now she was scared for her life too!"

"What??"

"The cheek of it!"

"Totally!"

I got on with my work and Marit made us both a coffee. I loved my new job!

I took Einar his coffee at the office building.

"How are you, Line?" he probed.

"You're meant to get back to normal after the funeral, aren't you?"

"There is no time limit for grief," he replied.

I sat with him and ate my sandwich. I was just finishing my coffee when Thor arrived at the office. I didn't want him in there, so I went outside to meet him.

"I didn't get a chance to see you yesterday," he began.

"It's no different to any other day," I replied coldly.

"I was hoping to go to the funeral with you, to support you."

"It's fine. Funerals are grim anyway. I wasn't there for long.

"So nothing significant happened yesterday?" he questioned me.

I shook my head.

"So, nobody went to the funeral with you? Comforted you?"

I looked at him blankly.

"Two coffee cups in the kitchen. Nobody came back with you? You went to bed early, so who was with you?"

"I always go to bed quite early these days. It's the sedatives."

"With you in another man's arms?"

"I've never taken someone to bed since I've been with you." I hoped that a response to that part of the questioning would keep him from probing more.

It was getting late and I needed to get back to work, so I apprehensively started taking a slow walk to Marit's.

"Look, I need to get back to work, Thor."

"I don't really care, Line, we need to talk!"

"So we'll talk tonight then," I suggested.

"No, because then I'll be at work.

"So I'll come and harass you when it's your break then?"

"Don't try and be smart, it doesn't suit you!" he blew up at me, passers-by turning to look at us, before he stormed off.

There would have been a time when that would affect me, but not these days. I literally didn't care anymore. I smiled as I entered the coffee shop and resumed work. Luckily, there were fans in the shop, but the customers in the queue were still struggling with the heat. The queue was building up even more during lunchtime.

"Is it worth me asking if any of the customers in the queue are planning to eat indoors? That way, I could find tables for them and take their orders?" I suggested once the rush was over. It wasn't a new concept by any means, but it could be a help. "Or maybe start two queues, so they can be next in line either of the queues? Maybe splitting the customers according to if they want food or drink maybe?"

"Hmmm..." Marit replied. "Two counters would require me to have at least another person here," she mused.

"It might be worth it if you consider how many customers are giving up on the queue?"

"It could be..." she followed me around as I cleaned. "Maybe the indoors versus outdoors? I'll have a think. Thanks, Line, sometimes you can just be too close to work things like this out."

I smiled. She returned to her counter, and I continued with my cleaning. I knew that I would remain in the customer area until I stopped taking the sedatives, but that was fine by me – I just hoped that it was fine by Marit. It was something that we could probably discuss during the appraisal. I continued to think of ideas for the rest of the shift.

Once I'd finished, I collected Einar's lunch and left for the day, with a passionfruit slushie. I'd never really liked passionfruit stuff, but these slushies were amazing. Einar had decided to have one too, so it was quite the juggle.

Einar was grateful for the slushie. I could see he was suffering with the heat. "I don't know how Mrs Johnsen did this," he mused.

"Well until H… Mrs Hansen attacked Aggie, there was no security on the door, so she could have them open on hot days like this."

"Even with that, August days, like today, are just so hot." He paused as he thought of Aggie. "I should have installed air con for her."

"I don't think it would have been necessary, so don't worry. There aren't enough hot days a year to justify it."

He wiped his forehead with a cloth he stored under the desk. He had already taken his jacket off. He stood up and walked over to the front door, opening it.

"Be damned with the security," he said.

"Just be aware of what is going on, one person has just been murdered here."

He nodded, his grey and black hair started to stick to his head. "Whoever killed Mrs Johnsen would be someone she knew, as she would have let them in."

I hadn't really thought of this before. There weren't any unknown guests that day. My head started filling with thoughts of someone she knew killing her. Was it even related to the building? Maybe Einar would be safe if it was Aggie that had been targeted? I rubbed my temples.

"Maybe I'll get a water cooler," Einar said to himself.

"Well, I'm off to the gym, which has air con!" I told him, standing up. "You wanna come?" I laughed.

"I'm not that hot!" he laughed as I left for a much-missed workout.

I checked into the gym but skipped the coffee, it was too hot. I saw some classes listed on the activities board, just behind the personal trainer who was at the counter. There was a spin class in about 20 minutes. I enquired about it. It was a cycling class and there were still places available. Excellent! I went into the changing rooms, had a quick shower and changed into the gym clothes that were stored in my locker. I checked that my money was still in there, which, of course, it was.

Satisfied with the cycling spin class, I showered and changed into my day clothes. On my way out (via coffee) I checked out the notice board for other sessions and made a note of those that I could attend, before or after work.

Once I was home, I had a glass of wine and a shower. I emptied my dirty clothes from the gym into the washing machine, and repacked my bag with clean clothes.

The wine and sedatives kicked in not long later, so I went to bed.

Heidi Hansen

Chapter 19 – A Fine Blue Line

I felt Thor get into bed last night, seemingly drunk, despite me being in a semi-deep sleep, and he was trying to wake me up. I remained as still as possible with the hope that he would just roll over and go to sleep. He continued to try and initiate sex with me. Despite my unconsciousness, he pushed further and further, until I woke up.

"What are you doing?" I whispered, not wanting to wake Kristian or the neighbours up.

"My conjugal rights," he replied.

"I'm trying to sleep," I replied.

"So?"

"So… stop it. At least aim to get permission first!"

"I'm your boyfriend, and you don't say no." He continued to try to take my pyjama shorts off.

"No! Is that clear enough?!"

He muttered something unintelligible, shrugged and rolled over.

I looked at the time on my phone, it was only 02:15. I quickly dressed in yesterday's clothes and left the flat.

At the gym, I had a couple cups of coffee, and had a little cry.

"Are you ok, miss?" one of the staff asked me.

"Yes, sorry." I tried a little smile.

He came over with a couple of tissues. "Thank you," I said.

I snapped myself out of it and proceeded to the changing rooms. I showered, to wash away the morning's actions and changed into my clean gym clothes. As I had a little extra time, I decided to have a turn on the treadmill and cross trainer. The latter took a little practice, but it all made me feel much better. There was a massive clock in the gym so I had no worries about being late for work.

An hour before I was due to start work, I showered and changed, and sat having a coffee while I thought things over. I realised that I had made little effort to find a new place to live, and now decided that I needed to step up a bit. I bought a newspaper on the way to work, which had local property listings.

"So I mulled over your ideas from yesterday, Line," Marit explained, shortly after I arrived. "Originally I thought that taking table orders would help, but I think that the queue would still be difficult." I felt deflated. "I thought about what you said about the two counters, and I think that might be the way forward. Two queues, rather than one."

I nodded and frowned simultaneously.

"I was worried about how many customers would order with you, and then run before they pay, though. Plus, I don't know how you would keep track…"

"How do you think we could split the queues?" I mused.

"Where that sign is in the corner," she pointed to the far corner, "there's a second door. A couple of signs and a bit of prompting from you should get people to know the new system."

I nodded.

"There are three people working here, aren't there?" Marit nodded. "Well," I continued, "you could be on the till for the takeaways, Frøya could be like a runner, fetching the food, and then I could tend to the customer area?"

"Ok, well have a think, and I will too."

I smiled and returned to my cleaning. Work was great, as it kept my brain too busy to think, but once I had my break, my brain was back to working overtime. I had no close friends, it seemed, as Bella didn't seem 'available', Marit was my boss, Erik was a no-no, and the only other people I had in my life were the Valle brothers. I could speak to Lillianne, I mused, but again, she could overreact to my detriment. I wished, for today only, to not have to take coffee to Einar, so I could try and get my head straight to focus on getting a new home, or working out how I could adjust my sleep pattern further so I didn't encounter Thor AT ALL.

I couldn't let Einar down, so I took a slow walk to Olsen Business Services. Einar smiled when he saw me, and I noticed lines on his face – worry lines or laughter lines? I doubted they were laughter lines. I handed him his coffee and sat with him, not really saying much at all.

"What's on your mind?" Einar had noticed my sadness.

"Nothing I can really talk to anyone about," I shrugged.

"Would have been easier to speak to Agnes about?" he said.

I thought about that briefly; no, I couldn't have spoken to Aggie about this particular incident. Sexual... abuse? Is that what it would be considered to be? I shook my head.

"No, I don't think I could have even talked to Aggie about it," I surmised.

"If it is something serious, you must talk to someone. There are some things that need to be sorted, no matter what."

I nodded. "I'm sorry I'm not being much company," I tried to smile, fighting back tears.

"You'd be surprised how great your company is."

This made me stop in my tracks. Maybe he needed me as much as I needed him.

"So, tell me a bit about yourself, Line," he probed. "Nothing related to how you feel now, just general things, like family, friends…"

"I'm not sure what is going on with my friends right now," I started. "I keep missing weekly get-togethers with them on Fridays. I feel like a crap friend." I opened up a little too much!

"It's Friday today," he announced, "So is it too late for you to sort it out tonight?"

"I hope to," I replied, "I think they are losing hope with me."

"Real friends won't think that or blame you," Einar announced.

I picked at my salmon sandwich, sighing deeply.

"Family?"

"My Papa is lovely. He used to be a schoolteacher but gave it all up to be a stay-at-home father. My mother is a pharmaceutical rep," I sighed. "I have an older sister called Lillianne," I concluded.

"Is your pappa planning to return to teaching now you have both grown up?"

I thought about this for a second. "I really don't know," I replied, smiling. "He spends most of his time cooking," I laughed. "When I was there the other week, he gave me batches of food to freeze."

"Lovely. Home-cooked foods are always the best!"

I nodded. I felt my phone buzz in my pocket for my alarm to remind me to go back to work.

"I have to go," I announced, "so sorry!"

"Don't be. Have fun at work, and I'll see you after? Or are you going to meet your friends?"

"I'll be here. Give me your lunch order!"

Back at work, I caught up with cleaning the customer area, and allowed my troubles to drift out of my mind once again. I chatted to customers, and work breezed by. Once it calmed down, my brain kicked in again. I was determined to not get upset again, so I tried to problem solve Marit's two-counter dilemma.

I looked at the tables as they slowly emptied after the lunchtime rush. How could I keep track of who orders what? A jar in the middle of the table with a wooden spoon inside, with numbers written on them, maybe? I think I'd been to another café and seen something similar.

It was soon time to finish work for the week. I felt sad, but at least I could be back in just a couple of days, and I could spend the weekend at the gym, along with flat-hunting and getting my brain in gear for the shop queue solution... I grabbed Einar's lunch and headed to the office building.

"Your turn," I announced.

Einar looked confused.

"Your turn, to tell me about yourself!"

"Well, you seem a bit happier," he announced, changing the subject.

"Not especially," I replied, "just keeping my mind busy."

A client came to his desk, so I busied myself on my phone. I had texts from Erik and Isabella.

'Hope u r having a good week. Not had chance to catch up with u since funeral' was from Erik.

I replied. 'Hey, sorry, I'm crap. Difficult few days. We'll have 2 catch up soon'.

'Guess u aren't coming out with us again this week? Hope to see u soon tho', from Bella. I didn't quite know how to respond to this. I pondered for a few minutes.

Einar's distraction had gone, so I lay my phone in my lap and turned my attention back to him. He told me that he had a wife and a daughter. Another client interrupted us, so I turned back to my phone.

'Hey Tinkerbell! I'll meet u @ the gym! Don't want to miss it 4 the world!' I replied to Isabella's message.

The office door buzzed again. It was Thor. I sighed to myself and said goodbye to Einar.

"Hi, Thor."

"Hi Line," Thor beamed at me.

I looked puzzled. "What do you want?" I asked him.

"Is that any way to greet the love of your life?"

"What do you want?" I repeated.

"Well, we will have to move out of the flat in a few weeks, so I thought we should probably check out some properties."

I really didn't want to move anywhere with him, but looking at some flats could work well for me. I nodded and he led me out. He got us a taxi and whisked me away to the first property. He retrieved the papers with the listings on, and pointed to what was a three-bedroomed house.

"We don't need three bedrooms," I attempted to explain.

"Shh, just look how lovely it is."

"I looked at the paper. "We can't afford it."

"Just try," he became agitated.

"Ok, what time is the estate agent coming then?" I looked at my phone, it was 16:28.

"Huh? No, there's no estate agents, we're just going to hope the tenant is in."

"What?? You can't do that!"

He continued to the door and knocked. Nobody answered.

"Ok, nobody is in, so we can just take a peek through the window…"

"No, we can't," I said, retreating swiftly.

I realised that the taxi was still outside the house. I approached the driver. "Did he not pay you?" I enquired.

"He said you will, once you have been to see a few properties."

That would cost an absolute fortune!

"C'mon!" Thor shouted. "You can't see it from all the way over there!"

I stormed up to him. "You can't do this, it must be illegal or something!"

"Maybe check with your boss on Monday then!"

He walked back to the taxi, me trying to keep up with his large strides, and we both got in. He gave the next address to the driver, and we were off again.

"I don't think it's wise for you to dress like that at work," he told me. "Hansen is a bit of a letch, there's way too much skin."

"He's not there at the moment," I picked my words very carefully.

"No?" he probed further.

I shook my head and looked down at the paper of property listings, indicating it was the end of the story on that matter.

We arrived at the next property, in a very pristine suburb somewhere. It was a block of apartments. The driver remained and we walked over to the intercom.

"Which number is it?" I asked him.

He shrugged. "No idea, thought you were the super sleuth!"

He pressed all the buttons for the flat intercoms. "Someone will buzz us in," he explained, and someone did.

"So I guess we don't have an appointment for here either?"

"No, but it looks like a great area and the apartment block common spaces seem nice and well-maintained."

I looked at him blankly.

"WHAT??!" he yelled at me.

"Why are we visiting the outside of properties? What does this achieve?"

"You are always so pessimistic?!" he continued.

"What can we do at these places? And how can we afford the taxi rides for it?!" I yelled back.

"FINE. We won't bother then! You'll have to either cancel the notice to our landlord or we'll have to refuse to leave?! HUH?"

"Neither solves our issues though, does it?"

"Well, it's *you* holding us back."

I looked at him blankly again. We got back into the taxi.

"How far away from the centre is this place, please?" I politely asked the driver.

He clicked his phone. "Five kilometres," he replied.

"Can we just go home now please?" I begged.

"Whatever!" Thor replied angrily.

I gave the driver the address and we were soon home.

He bolted out of the taxi and was upstairs in a couple of strides. By the time I had paid the taxi driver, using my wages from the café and reached our door, he'd slammed it, so I needed to rummage through my bag for my key. He had stormed into my bedroom, and I was left in the living area with Kristian, who was playing games on the TV. I sat down at the breakfast bar and checked my phone. There was still time to go out with the girls, but I didn't feel emotionally up to it.

"What we got for dinner?" Kris asked me.

"I've no idea. We all work, so maybe we should take it in turns. You've had a day off today, haven't you? So how are your cooking skills?"

"We pay to live here now, so you should make dinner!"

"We all pay the same to live here, so why should it be just me to cook?"

"Well, you're a woman!" he replied.

I stared at him.

"You cooked for us when we weren't paying, so you should cook now."

"Surely that's another reason for us all to share the cooking then? In fact, seeing as I have done so much cooking in the past, it must be time for me to have a break from it?!"

"This is bullshit!" he responded.

I didn't care anymore. I was tired, physically and emotionally. I wanted a shower and bed, but Thor was still in the bedroom. I poured myself a large glass of wine and took my meds. I approached the bedroom and opened the door. Thor was lying on the bed, staring at the ceiling. I chose to ignore him and had a shower. He was still there when I came out, but I was so tired that I just climbed into the bed on my side and promptly fell asleep.

Heidi Hansen

Chapter 20 - Time and Again

The next morning, I awoke feeling quite groggy. Thor wasn't beside me, so that was a bonus! I rolled out of bed and had a shower, choosing more pyjamas for the day at home. I went to the kitchen for coffee and found the whole living area trashed. Beer cans, pizza boxes and general rubbish. There were extra covers on the floor next to the sofa, so it seemed that Thor had slept there last night. I no longer cared, luckily.

I sat at the breakfast bar to drink my coffee, as I could smell the boys from there as it was, which would be nothing compared to sitting on the sofa. 'Let them live in their own squalor', I thought.

I pulled out the newspaper that I'd bought yesterday, and turned to the property section. I was happy to look for one-bedroom places, or even a studio. I used to love this flat, but knew I couldn't love it anymore as it just reminded me of these times I was experiencing now. It was time for a fresh start. The locations or prices of each property were unsuitable for me. Sure, I could probably cycle to work quite easily now…

Days off were boring, so I got dressed and retrieved the money envelope that the boys had paid me out of the cupboard. It was empty. I remember them giving me 5,000 kroner. When was that? We had used some for the food that week, but there should still be some money left. They clearly hadn't paid for a few weeks and had been helping themselves to the cash in there. I wanted to rant, wanted to confront them when they got home, but what was the point? They weren't going to pay, it seemed. I had planned to go food shopping today, but there was no point now. I decided to just feed myself, screw them! I decided to hit the gym, knowing that I could grab some of the stored money from my locker to pay for my food.

At the gym, I spent the whole time thinking about foods that I could buy myself that the boys didn't like. Anything healthy, was the general theme! Fruit, vegetables and muesli seemed to be at the top of my list. I'd stick to coffee at the gym or at work, leaving them with none. At the flat, I'd resort to fruit juice or my lemon tea. Lunches would be mainly at work, and the dinners I could grab from a shop on the day, after work, so they wouldn't have access to them. I decided to not use the money from my locker – that would be for the rent. So I'd just use my weekly wages for my daily food as and when I needed it. Not that there was much left after the previous day's taxis.

The boys didn't even know that I was now being paid weekly, so as far as they were concerned, I was out of money by now. They had left me with no food and no money. I grew angrier at this and fought back tears. I needed to become stronger again, physically *and* mentally!

Enough! NO MORE SELF-PITY!

I had a couple of cups of coffee at the gym after I had showered and changed, then headed home. The coffee shop was rammed, so I just waved as I walked by, and popped into the supermarket to see what food I fancied for the day. I opted for granola, fruit and yogurt. Mmm perfect! Back at home, I split it all between two bowls, so that I could just grab the next one if Kristian was asleep later.

I checked my phone as I was eating, and found a text message from Bella. 'Where u @? U said u wud be here?'. Damn, I felt awful.

'Sorry Tink, really struggling with the boys rn. Not doing it on purpose, pinky promise xx'.

Erik had replied to my last text. 'Ok Miss U! Not wrkn Sun if that's any gd?'. It had been a while since he had called me Miss U – it stood for Miss Unsophisticated, which was more or less what Mamma had called me when we were at the restaurant where he worked – the first time we met. The first time he had called it me by text, I had almost misinterpreted it! I missed him, I realised more each day.

'Deffo meet up 2moz, any ideas?', I replied. I didn't want to seem too keen or desperate, a friendship with him would be great.

The next text was from Pappa. 'Hey Bumblebee, how are you? Hopefully keeping busy and happy. Call me anytime'.

Did I want to let him know how unhappy I was? I could do with some form of venting, maybe to help me convert to my new 'no messing' attitude. There were of course some subjects that I couldn't discuss with him. As much as I enjoyed my time in Bergen, I was invested in work, and Erik. However, these were probably the only things holding me together right now, too. I didn't trust myself to lose my façade over the phone, so chose to respond to his text instead.

'Hey Pappa. All good here, work is going great. Joined a gym too. Will chat soon xx'. That'd do it!

Knowing that Thor would be home about midnight and then in bed a couple of hours later, I decided to tweak my sleep pattern slightly, going to bed with the aim to get up by the time he was due to come to bed. That meant that I'd need to be going to sleep quite soon, though, so I got rid of the rest of my coffee in the pot, washed it up and converted to decaf tea and wine!

I had a shower, dressed into clean pyjamas and settled myself into bed.

~

The next morning, I woke up just as Thor had come to bed. I got up swiftly, and walked over to my chair to sit there instead. I plugged my earphones in and watched videos on my phone. The little breeze from the window was welcomed. I wondered where I would go today, and whether it would be with Erik or not. I didn't want to rely on Erik, or build any hopes up. Not caring about Thor sleeping or not, I boiled the kettle for my lemon tea and went for a shower. As expected, he was snoozing by the time I returned to my tea and chair. I could hear Kristian in the living room playing a combat game on the console. Waiting for him to go to sleep would take a while. I was in no rush. I was awake and happy enough. A loud expletive came from his direction later, followed by a crash, presumably the controller for Kris' console. He banged around the kitchen for a few minutes then returned to the sofa. I recognised the squeak of the sofa when someone sat on it. It was even more annoying when they were playing computer games, bouncing up and down. I rolled my eyes, and plugged my earphones back in. I was itching to get to the gym, and desperate for some caffeine, so I bit the bullet, grabbed my things and left.

It was still really quiet as I walked through the city, with almost every shop being closed. Luckily, the gym was 24/7, and the coffee aroma drew me in before I reached the door. The staff were getting used to me and greeted me. I started with a couple of coffees before showering and changing, ready for the equipment.

The cross trainer was my new favourite, closely followed by the exercise bike. I 'climbed' for imaginary kilometres, and I felt great. I lost track of how long I was working out, but it had been alone. After I showered and dressed, I emerged from the changing room to come face-to-face with one of the staff.

"I think you have slipped through the net, somehow, Miss Larsen," the man started.

"Ok?" I replied, confused.

"You have been drinking coffee just here," he gestured to the little coffee machine area.

"Oh, no! Was I not meant to?"

"Come this way," he replied, and walked away from the main doors, opening a little door next to both changing rooms. I watched the man, who was probably the same age as me. He was tall, with very muscly arms, which housed a couple of tribal tattoos.

"There's a whole members' lounge here," he explained, smiling.

The whole room was amazing. So comfortable, with pots of free coffee! There was a TV, and a variety of magazines too!

"Sorry, we should have told you from the very beginning," he said, and left me to it. I poured myself a cup of coffee and relaxed into one of the soft chairs.

This was a game-changer – this was what was going to get me through all this.

I had decided that midday would be the cut-off time for caffeine moving forward. This was to ensure that I slept without any *interference*. I also decided that now was the time to wean myself off the sedatives. It had been a few weeks now, and I was in too much of a deep sleep while I was taking them. I needed to be alert.

The heat hit me when I left the gym. They had air con there, so it was easy to be blissfully unaware of the outside temperature. The new members' lounge had a water cooler, so I had filled up my water bottle before leaving. I must have been there quite a while, as it was now light and there were people milling around. I walked to Marit's and found that it wasn't too busy. I plonked my bag and water bottle on a chair and approached the counter. There was a young woman working I hadn't met before.

I treated myself to a strawberry smoothie, as it was now 'no caffeine' time. I was busy licking my spoon when I was approached.

"Good afternoon, Line," Erik beamed at me.

'I should never have let you down', I wanted to say. I secretly knew it was too late.

"Hello, Erik," I replied, smiling at him.

"Thought I'd come in for a slushie, then I saw you!"

"Marit's slushies are AMAZING!"

He smiled and went to the counter. I pulled some money out of my purse and followed him, butting in to pay for the drinks before he had the chance.

"Hey!" he protested.

"You bought mine last time," I explained, "so it's my turn to return the favour."

He shook his head, smiling, and returned to the table.

"So what is your plan for the day?" he enquired.

I shrugged. "I thought I might go to Frogner Park, where I went to recently. There's like a water thing there, and there's lots of kids there usually."

"'Water thing'?" he laughed. "Kids?"

I laughed. "Yeahhh, I get your point. I accidentally bumped into the Hansens last time I was there! So yeah, I need new suggestions."

"Well, there's been this one place I've wanted to visit for a while..."

"Ok...?"

"We'll go when you have finished your smoothie," he smiled at me.

Armed with slushies, we left Marit's and I followed Erik to see where our destination would be. First stop was the bus station.

We passed some beautiful scenery during this bus journey to the mystery location. It reminded me why I love Norway so much.

After about 45 minutes we arrived in **Drøbak**, about 30 miles south west of Oslo, which had a beautiful harbour and marina. We strolled along the marina, popping into some shops on the way. We stopped for some lunch, after Erik heard my stomach complaining. We slurped on the creamy fish soup that we ordered, perfect for the lovely summer's day.

I talked to him about the plans for the café.

"How about an app?" he suggested.

"An app?" I repeated.

"Yes, you can get apps where people can order from their tables and it goes straight to the counter. It should be a quick thing; add all the items on that are on the menu, along with the prices, and they order and pay from the table."

"Ohh, that sounds really good. I was thinking about painting numbers of wooden spoons to indicate what the table number is. for the customers *and* for us."

"Hmmm, not bad," he nodded. "Think about the theme of the café. It's not a 'greasy spoon' like some cafés are, it's fresher."

"Ok?" I queried.

"Remember that shop we went to where they had jars with seashells and glass stones in? Well that would be good for this area, but how about, say, fake fruit in jars, which have numbers on?"

"Oh, I like your thinking!"

"I'd suggest going somewhere a little cheaper for them though, rather than here. It's a tourist kinda place, so the prices are hiked right up."

I nodded. "You are just brilliant!" I smiled at him.

"Of course," he replied, coolly slipping his sunglasses back on.

~

After lunch, Erik took me to Drøbak Akvarium. I had never been to an aquarium before, and it was the most beautiful place that I had ever seen. There were floor-to-ceiling glass stands, with fish in, of course. Fish of all colours, just a few millimetres away. A glass archway that we walked under was fascinating. Different species of crab and lobsters made me feel guilty for eating them. Different octopusses, or is it octopi? Whatever the correct collective term was, they were so strange to look at. We were allowed to touch some in a little rockpool that they had created. Children ran around excitedly, and it was only because I was older that I didn't do the same.

I wanted to stay there forever, with Erik, forever. I didn't know if he felt the same way, and indeed, I think he assumed that I was happily living with Thor. We left the aquarium just before it closed, and arrived at just the right time to catch the bus home. I leaned on Erik for the journey home, and held his hand; he didn't resist.

As we arrived back in Oslo, I felt that I shouldn't try to push him further by kissing him, but there was a long pause, with locked eyes, before we went our separate ways home. It was way past my preferred bedtime, but I didn't feel as tired as I should. I looked at the photos that I had taken during the day, as I uploaded them into a separate photo app that Thor didn't know about. I felt sneaky, and realised it could be a bad mark on my record, to add to the one where I cheated on Erik. It seemed like I was becoming a serial adulterer, and perhaps that was true.

<u>Chapter 21 - Driftwood</u>

Fully aware that Monday was the brothers' day off, I still crept around the flat to get ready for work. I had woken up later than I had wanted. I grabbed my yogurt fruit mix from the fridge, and returned to my bedroom to sit on my chair. I kept my phone visible so that I could track the time. I risked a shower, hoping that Thor wouldn't wake, and crept out of the flat as soon as I was ready to go.

I arrived at work just in time. Marit was there already, of course. I helped myself to a coffee and sat in the staff area for a few minutes.

"Did you have any ideas about the new layout?" she asked me, when she came to join me for coffee.

"Yes," I replied enthusiastically. "I spoke to someone in the catering industry, and they talked to me about using an app. Some restaurants, cafés, bars and all that, have an app that people can download. They click on the menu, add their table number and pay via this app. So they can sit straight away, and order. There's no risk of them running off without paying, and the app will be on their phone for next time they visit. The app, with your brand details and logo, will be there, just waiting to make eye contact with them."

"WOW! That sounds great. I'm not sure I'll have time to upload all of that…"

"Don't worry I'll have a play around and see what I can do. I 'll take a menu home with me. If you send me your branding and logo, I can sort."

"WOW!" she repeated.

"I won't do anything official until you are happy with it," I continued to explain.

"What about those who don't want to use their phone?"

"All tables can have menus on them, with something that has the table number on it, which I have a couple of ideas about, and I can take their orders or they can come to the counter."

"Well, that gives me quite a lot to think about. Thanks so much, Line, you could be the breath of fresh air I've been wanting all this time."

"Just fresh eyes," I replied.

I drank the rest of my coffee and headed to the customer area to give it a clean, ready for the day. Marit opened the doors and the first few customers started to arrive. I had nothing to do at this point, as I still wasn't allowed to use the machinery, or sharp knives, so I sat and started to write out ideas for the re-jig of the shop, drawing a *very* rough floor plan. I popped back and forth with the cleaning and planning until my lunch break.

I took a coffee round to Einar, and excused myself, for now, so I could pop to a couple of shops to get some table decorations, based on my observations of the coffee shop. The coffee shop had quite an industrial/minimalistic theme to it, with wooden and metal accessories, so of course floral pieces wouldn't be any good. I could stay with just industrial looks, or introduce a colour. The best bet, I decided, was to buy with a couple of ideas in mind. The focus of the coffee shop was freshness, as I discussed with Erik yesterday. Coffee beans maybe, in jars? I hunted the city for inspiration without breaking the bank.

I found some great, vintage-looking mason jars and some classy number stickers. In the nearby supermarket, I found some cheap coffee beans, and some bags of berry pot pourri. I popped in to see Einar again and to get his food order for later, then returned to Marit's, promising to spend more time with him after work.

The shop was busy, so I spent most of my time catching up with the tables until the lunchtime rush had passed. Then I went through to the staff area with a coffee and worked on the jars. I only had two jars at first, to see what she liked. If she didn't like either, then I'd keep them myself!

They looked great, and I placed the two on different tables, and popped a menu next to them. There seemed to be something missing from it. I spotted a couple of little trays under the counter and slipped them under the jars. I grabbed a couple of spoons and walked over to the tables with Marit.

"What do you think?" I asked nervously. "If you don't like one of the designs, it could be swapped with spoons?"

"I love it, Line, they both look great. Is it possible to find smaller jars for the spoons. Have a look in the stockroom, actually, there might be something there. We could alternate the jars; one table coffee, one fruit, etc. etc.?"

"Most definitely. I'll take a look in the stock room tomorrow morning?" I replied.

"That would be great. Can you give some thought to signs for the two queues?"

"I'll have a think," I replied, scooping up Einar's lunch and waving goodbye.

I felt great.

I handed over Einar's food and sat in the reception area for a bit. Despite Thor being at the flat all day, I still intended to go to the gym! In fact, that was more reason to go. Olsen's Business Services always had a stack of newspapers at the end of the desk, and I asked if I could borrow one.

"What's new today then? Is the newspaper telling you any truths?" he probed.

"Do they ever?" I laughed. "I'm just looking at the properties to rent."

"What kind of property are you looking for?"

"Just something small really," I replied. "Studio or one bed ideally. Can't afford much though, and the issue seems to be that expensive places are in the city, whereas cheaper ones are quite a distance."

"I have properties," he announced.

I raised my eyebrows. "Do you?" I replied, surprised.

"Yes, not just this place," he explained. "There's a couple of vacant one-bedroomed places here in the city. What kind of price can you afford?"

"I'm currently paying around 10,000 a month. I know it's not a lot, but I only get minimum wage."

He paused for a few seconds. I looked back down in the newspaper to keep searching.

"I have one in Frogner, and one in Holmendammen. They are both one-bedroomed?"

"How much and what do you require?"

"Require? Normally I ask for a month's rent up front and the same amount as a deposit, but I'm sure we could come to some kind of arrangement. Ah, I mean that in a 'friend' way, not in a 'put you up in your own apartment and you pay 'in kind''!" he laughed nervously. "Shall I start that again?"

I laughed. "So you could ask for less deposit, for example?"

"Yes, if you need to."

"Ok, will I be able to see them at some point?"

"We can go once I lock up here, if you like?"

"That sounds great." I sat in the reception area and sipped my coffee, waiting for him to finish.

He locked up and gestured toward his car. "They are both walkable, but it'll be easier to go from one to the other by car."

I nodded and got into the passenger side. It was a very nice car. Very clean, very fast. Smelled like a new car. We were at the first property in just a couple of minutes. He opened his glove compartment and pulled out a keyring full of keys. He got out and opened the door for me. 'Old skool' I thought. We entered building and it smelled like cleaning products.

"The building communal areas are cleaned daily. This apartment has furniture included, but if you don't need it, then I can put it all into one of my other apartments."

We climbed the stairs to the top floor. Einar was struggling, but I managed the incline easily. He opened the door and allowed me to go in. I had a good look round.

"This one is 11,549 a month, but includes internet," he announced.

"What area is this one?" I enquired.

"This is the Holmendammen one," he replied.

The furniture was nice, but I wasn't keen on the bathroom and very small kitchen. It would do, if the other one wasn't any better, but I was willing to check out another one.

"I think I will need furniture, and the things that are here would be very useful." I thought about the sofa and bed that I wouldn't like to take with me.

"Ok," he said, "that's not a problem. If there's other furniture that you would need, then I could sort that too. Did you want to view the next one?"

"Yes please, if that is ok?"

"Of course," he smiled, and we descended the stairs at a faster pace than we had come up them.

We arrived at the one in Frogmore, and I could see the park I had been to. This property looked better from the outside, but that wasn't what mattered the most.

"It has an intercom service," he pointed to the metal box on the wall. "There's a lift in this one too!"

"Sold!" I laughed.

We were there in seconds, and the place had a nice, airy feel to it. It looked very empty right now, but could be interpreted as a blank canvas.

"This one is 11,495 Kroner a month," he informed me. "but it needs some cosmetic modernisation to it, so I'd happily reduce it to 10,000 a month if you would decorate it nicely."

I really liked this place. "Would it be possible to have some of the furniture from the first place in this one instead?" I enquired.

"Most definitely. What would you need?"

"Sofa, bed, double if possible?"

"Washing machine and dryer?" he asked. "I could get them plumbed in for you."

It was a great offer. There was already a cooker there too. "How about a fridge?" Had I asked for too much.

"I can get you a fridge freezer, there's a lovely one in Koselig," he offered.

"Are you sure?" I asked.

"Most definitely."

"When... when could I move in?"

"You like it then?" I nodded. "Anytime after tomorrow. I can get my people in to move the furniture in."

"Can I do the weekend?" I asked.

He nodded. "I can get the paperwork ready for you before then."

"Deposit?"

"Can you manage the month's rent in advance?"

I tried to remember how much money I had stored in my locker at the gym. I was sure I still had about 40,000 kroner, but still had to pay for the final month's rent, which would leave me with 30,000.

"Yes, I can," I replied, grinning with excitement.

"It's a deal!" he said, holding out his hand to shake mine.

I had a final look round, and smiled even more. It would be great. We left the building and returned to the car.

As he drove me home, he pointed out all the other properties he had, but not in a smug way, just for conversation. He pointed to the building opposite my current flat. I remembered the flash from a camera came from there.

"You'll never guess who rents the apartment I own in that building!"

"I give up!" I replied.

"Mr Hansen! I doubt it will be long, seeing as he doesn't want to 'do business' with me anymore!"

"WOW! I didn't realise he was that close to me!"

Inside, my mind was working overtime. HANSEN!! HANSEN, with his stupid camera at Frogner Park! I kept it together until I got out of the car, outside the flat. I smiled at Einar and proceeded upstairs. I took a deep breath until I got inside, trying to control my emotions. I desperately wanted to contact Erik to tell him about it, but also had to deal with the Valle brothers. On the plus side, this would be the last Monday I'd have to deal with this! I still had Friday, but could do my best to avoid them then too. I'd need to look at getting a truck or something, to move what things I was taking with me. I had to put all of this on the back burner for now.

"Who was that?" Thor was on me as soon as I walked in.

"Huh?" I replied.

"The snazzy red car. Who was it?"

"Oh, that was Mr Olsen."

"And why is *Mr Olsen* driving you home?"

'Think, Line!', I desperately needed a decent answer.

"Mrs Hansen was causing me some issues after work."

"Bitch!"

"Huh?" I replied.

"How dare she mess with you!"

"It's over now, chill!" I responded.

"Chill?!" he raised his voice.

"I can handle her!"

"If I see her…" Kristian piped up.

"It's not an issue," I reiterated. "Drop it!"

I proceeded to the bedroom and made myself a cup of lemon tea. The curtains were closed – one of my pet peeves, so I opened them and opened my window. There was a slight breeze, and it was very refreshing, as was the tea I was drinking.

'HANSEN! The Hansens live in that building opposite me, so it must be him that's taking photos of me!' I text Erik when I was a little more chilled. I still felt shaky inside, though. I closed my eyes and focussed on controlling my breathing.

I had so much planning to do, I wasn't sure where to start! I decided that today I would focus on the inventory; what I would take and what would have to stay.

'Breathe, Line, breathe', I thought to myself.

Tomorrow I would focus on finances.

I started by looking around the bedroom. I was determined to take my curtains; I'd loved them from the beginning. Bedding I would take, washing it all before I used it. All 'hard' furniture would have to stay. This was a similar pattern throughout the flat, except my chair! How would I move my chair?! Would I have to leave it behind? Could I train myself to stop loving it? This was already getting stressful, but I knew I'd just need to keep my eyes on the prize!

Chapter 22 – Forever Not Yours

If I was in a movie right now, the song in the background would be 'Walking on Sunshine'! I was so happy today! The weather was a little cooler, I'd solved the riddle of the secret stalker (although I didn't know how to deal with it). I had finally nodded off, despite the excitement, and had woken up just before Thor came to bed. I had even managed to sit in my chair with a cup of tea and a book beforehand, and ensured him that I'd be in bed soon. That had been a pure lie, obviously! *What's good for the goose* and all that! I'd managed to leave the flat as soon as he had gone to sleep, whilst Kris was still up, playing on his game. He was so in the zone that he didn't even notice. This didn't mean that I could let my guard down, I wasn't free yet.

The gym was what I now considered comfort, as I curled up on the sofa with coffee, watching TV. It was a Valle-free area! I had a second coffee before showering and changing. I checked the money in my locker and wrote the amount into my personal organiser. I then headed to the gym for some cycling, walking, rowing and climbing. Afterwards, I had a shower and changed into my work clothes, then went back to the lounge for more coffee.

I arrived at work early, so I sat on the pavement outside until Marit was there.

"You seem different today, Line," she commented.

I nodded, "I am different."

She paused for a second, looking at me before smiling and continuing to clean the coffee machine. I rummaged through the stockroom to look for something to put spoons in to dress the tables. I found some little silver-coloured metal milk jugs. I popped them in the dishwasher for later, when the shop was quiet.

I checked my phone when I got my break, and found a response from Erik.

'Don't worry, we'll sort! Xx'.

I visited Einar, to deliver his coffee during my lunch break.

"Are you still happy with moving into the Frogner apartment this weekend?" he asked.

I panicked a little. "Yes, there's no problem with it, is there?"

"Oh, no, it's all ok. I'm getting my lawyer to draw up the contract and my men to move the furniture today."

"As long as Mr Hansen isn't the lawyer?" I half-laughed.

"Oh, no, mine is decent!"

We both laughed, and I breathed a secret sigh of relief.

"Is cash ok for the rent or do you prefer digital payments?"

"Do you not have a bank account?" he queried.

"I do, but I now get paid in cash. I can deposit the money into the bank if you prefer?"

"Cash is fine," he confirmed. "I was just curious."

I left for the time being and returned to work. The day moved on swiftly, which was good as tiredness set in quite early, and I contemplated skipping the gym today. I upped the caffeine intake to get me through the rest of my shift, and made my afternoon visit to Einar shorter than usual. Although I knew that the boys didn't leave for work until around 4 p.m., I just couldn't keep my eyes open.

As I walked through the door of the flat, the noise was tremendous. Kris was playing video games on the TV, with a mass of youths! I just dismissed it, making a mental note to apologise to the landlord and neighbours. I proceeded to the bedroom to find Thor in bed with a random blonde girl.

"W…what are you doing here?!" Thor blurted, as the girl covered herself up.

"Get out!" I yelled at the girl.

She obliged, stumbling around the bedroom to look for her clothes. I returned to the living area and yelled at them to all get out too. They laughed and carried on gaming. I turned to the faithful switching off the power at the fuse box and they all left, moaning at Kris.

"What the hell do you think you are doing?!" Kris raged at me.

"You have no right to invite all these people around *my* flat!" I yelled back at him.

"THIS IS OUR FLAT!" he yelled back at me.

Thor appeared out of the bedroom, now fully dressed.

I lowered my tone. "We have to be out of the flat in three weeks. You have two weeks to get this flat spotless, otherwise the deposit won't be refunded."

"So," Kris said. "That's your problem, not ours. You can't kick us out!"

"Oh, I can!"

I stood at the front door until they left for work 45 minutes later. I needed a new plan to kick them out. My tiredness had diminished slightly, and I promptly stripped the bed completely, to wash that blonde, and all that had happened, off it.

The whole flat was a pigsty, but I stood by my demand for them to get the place sorted in the next two weeks. It was the best I could do. I couldn't keep cleaning the place over and over again, just for them to trash it again. The whole place smelled like pizza and feet; I heaved at the thought of it all. I put clean covers on the bed, had a shower and went to bed.

I had a sleepless night, well, evening, I guess. I realised that I hadn't taken my sedatives. Taking them now would cause me to sleep in too much, so I pulled a secret bottle of wine out of the back of my closet and swigged most of it, before laying down again.

Chapter 23 – Butterfly Butterfly

Life returned to semi-normality once I had spent a whole day at work, although I did miss the morning gym session due to oversleeping. Any time spent with Thor, I had managed to numb my feelings as I secretly counted down to the weekend.

I had bought some clear plastic bags to store the majority of the soft furnishings and clothes in, only using boxes to store things like the coffee machine, which I would pad out with the remaining soft items. I knew there was no point doing any clearouts of rubbish, as the boys would just trash it again.

I'd upped my caffeine intake, and my body seemed to go into flight mode, which kept the adrenaline flowing. I kept myself busy with work, and the gym, and continued to alternate my sleeping with Thor's. He obviously knew that I wasn't happy with him, seeing as I'd just caught him in my bed with another woman, and he had started tidying the flat a little. I noted it but chose to not use positive reinforcement for this; it was too little, too late.

On Wednesday, Marit informed me that she wasn't sure about the milk jugs for the spoon storage and would continue to give them out with the customer's drinks. Frøya designed some fantastic signage for inside and outside. I worked on the app in the gym lounge. It all seemed quite easy to sort, and I could set up without it going live - before Marit approved. It looked like it could be adapted for customers to place orders for collection too – I made a mental note to mention that too.

I fluttered around the customer area like I was a butterfly, or walking on air. I had developed a bit of rapport with some of the regular customers too, which was great. I felt more liked, if that makes sense? I'd been in a completely different bubble before I started working at Marit's. With the exception of Aggie, it was just Hansen and the Valle boys, which was all so negative.

Einar brought all the paperwork with him for my new home and presented it to me when I visited with his lunch order. I read through and signed it with no issues. I promised him the money tomorrow, making a mental note to withdraw it from my locker in the morning, before work. I didn't want to sort it today, as I felt too much at risk with having it in the flat.

"If you need ANYTHING sorting out for the apartment, just let me know, Line," Einar announced.

"Do I need to start calling you Mr Olsen again?" I half-joked.

"No, no," he laughed.

I left him when he closed the office building and headed for the gym. I followed the usual routine there, and then returned to the flat. The boys had made even more effort to tidy the flat, and some cleaning appeared to be done too!

~

Thursday was equally non-eventful.

Marit loved the app, "Line, it all looks so professional. Is it ok for me to check it out in more detail tonight?"

I nodded and sent her the link. "The admins of the app can be given to anyone you choose. All admins can have different roles too; so, for example, you can set it so that I can only see orders, but someone else could change anything on it, as an example."

She nodded, and swiped and clicked the 'viewable content'. "I really love it. You are so clever, and so valuable to the team. I'm so glad that you came to work with me."

I felt quite warm inside when she said that – working *with* her, not *for* her.

She told me all about the plans for the rearrangement of the shop. As she was open every day, she knew she would have to work after hours to get it in place and we set the relaunch date for next Monday, as it was a fresh week and fresh month. I was so excited.

She did ask if I could come in during the weekend to help set it up, and I explained that I'd try, but that I was moving to a new flat, "It's low-key for now." She looked at me, confused and intrigued. "I'll explain it more on Monday."

I paid Einar the first month's rent for my new apartment and he gave me the keys. Everything was falling into place. I'd leave the booking of the taxi to the day, as it would depend when everything was ready and the current flat was clear of boys. They do work weekends, but if Thor becomes suspicious of anything, he may make an exception!

Heidi Hansen

Chapter 24 – Keeper of the Flame

I woke up just before the boys came home for work. Sleep didn't come as easily this week, partly because I'd 'gone cold turkey' with the sedatives, and partly because I was too focused on ensuring that everything would flow as planned. I sat in my chair with my tea and retrieved my personal organiser from my bag to check the progress so far.

Tenancy Agreement – done.

Keys to new place – done.

That appeared to be everything, so far. The remaining items were:

Pack all soft furnishings – almost all done, and enough bags to complete.

Book taxi.

Arrange for chair to be moved.

Change locks to flat when there's one week left to clean.

Hand new keys back to current landlord.

I was sure to tuck the organiser back into my bag before Thor came in. I already had my earphones in, and a book with me ready to grab to look busy, to hopefully avoid any conversation with him. It didn't work.

"Was the cleaning ok for you?" he asked, pulling one of my earphones away.

I nodded. I didn't want to push it by pointing out stuff that still needed to be sorted. "Yes, thank you."

I'd learned to be vocal with discussions, to avoid further repercussions of 'clearly being in a bad mood'.

"Are you coming to bed?" he continued.

"I will soon, hopefully. I've stopped taking the sedatives, so sleep is problematic lately," I over-explained.

Should I have told him that much? Probably not, but nothing could be taken back now.

"Completed?" he queried.

I nodded again. "Yeah."

"Did the doctor just stop supplying them?"

"I just got sick of them," I replied, again wishing I'd said something different, before he even responded.

"You can't just stop using them, just like that."

"I've got an appointment next week," I lied.

"When?"

I groaned inside. "Not sure, off the top of my head."

"Well can't you keep taking them until you see him?"

"I don't have any left," I lied further.

"Well, surely you can call the surgery to get an emergency prescription?"

"I'll ring them later."

"If Hansen doesn't let you off work to go to an appointment, let me know and I'll…"

I stood up. "I'm going for a shower," I announced, walking off in the middle of his rant.

After I showered and dressed, I sat in the bathroom for a while, hoping that he'd be asleep once I re-emerged. When I was confident that he was asleep, I crept into the kitchen using the shared bathroom door, and grabbed my water bottle out of the fridge. There was an envelope on the breakfast bar, addressed to me. Inside was 5,000 kroner. The message on the envelope read:

Here's some money for food. Sorry it's been a little sparse lately, I've been saving for something special. See you later. Thor xxx.

I checked the contents, stuffed the envelope into my gym bag and left. I had ensured that I had packed clothes for the girls' night later that evening, as well as clean gym clothes and work clothes. I contemplated taking the dirty clothes to my new home, but wasn't sure if I'd have time. There was no rush, I suppose.

I was so excited that I only managed one coffee before my workout. I processed the details of the finances in my head as I walked several miles on the treadmill. The money remaining in the locker from Mamma would cover removal costs and possibly pay for any decorating that I needed to do, although part of me wanted to pay her back. I obviously hadn't even told them that I was moving, in fact, nobody except for Einar knew. I couldn't risk anyone passing the information onto the Valles. I continued to calculate my finances while I climbed on the cross trainer, realising that the new apartment wasn't much more expensive than the current one, and I'd managed fine before the brothers moved in. I thought back to those times when I lived on my own and my excitement grew. It was going to be great. A slightly different area of the city to explore.

I had a couple of coffees after I'd showered and changed, and relaxed in the members' lounge for a while, trying to keep myself calm. I had a busy day with work, so I didn't have to worry about keeping my mind busy, and tomorrow… I'd be moving out!! I just needed to get through the time between going home after the night out, and when the boys went to work. I could even sleep during that time!

Work flew by, and it was during the afternoon that I had the unwelcome visitors of the Hansens. They clearly hadn't known that I was working there, but Kenneth took great pride in mocking me the whole time they were there, which they seemed to decide would be indoors, to gloat at me the whole time. I smiled sweetly and showed how happy I was to work there, conversing with the regular customers. Heidi didn't look especially happy, and I did think it was quite strange to see them both together.

"Well done, you!" Marit praised me, once they'd left, for remaining calm despite the married couple's visit.

I smiled. "All in a day's work!"

After work, I sat with Einar for a bit, bubbling with excitement again. I hadn't eaten all day, partly through the butterflies in my stomach, partly to allow room for the meal later tonight. We used to switch the restaurant/cuisine weekly so I didn't know what we would be eating tonight, but I didn't care. I would tell everyone what had been happening, and would tell them about moving to a new apartment. I may even have a moving-in party! I hoped that they would forgive me for my absence.

I wanted to leave the office building a little earlier today to avoid Thor's regular intervening habit, so said goodbye to Einar and left. Immediately I was accosted by Heidi, who seemed to have been waiting for me. She backed me up against the wall aggressively, by closing in on the space between us.

"What are you going to do about Kenneth?" she snarled.

"What do you mean?" I replied, confused.

"He is going to kill me, Line!" her voice rose.

While I didn't believe her, I wanted to appease her. "Just don't rile him," I suggested. "What is he so agitated about, that makes you think he'll...hurt you?"

"Well, you saw from your colleague's death that she hadn't done much wrong. He just has a short fuse. He isn't outwardly violent or angry, but he stores it up inside."

I'd always seen him more vindictive verbally than violent in the past, whereas Heidi had shown these traits. I still believed it was her that had murdered Aggie.

"Is there anything that you have done to trigger him? Does he have a record of violence in the past?"

She shook her head.

"Just be pleasant to him?" I concluded.

"You need to help me, Line!" she pleaded with me, putting less distance between us.

"OI!" a voice shouted. "Leave my wife alone!"

Surprisingly, it was Thor. I was more disturbed that he was saying I was his wife than Heidi's intimidation tactics.

He ran over to me, Kristian straggling behind, and Heidi moved away from me.

"What do you think you are doing?!" he growled at her.

"I was just talking to her," Heidi responded.

"Well, leave her alone!"

Einar appeared from the reception area.

"Are you ok, Miss Larsen?" he enquired.

I nodded. He turned to Heidi.

"Are you ok, Mrs Hansen?"

She nodded, and opened her mouth ready to speak.

"Heidi, get in here, NOW!" someone shouted from a car nearby.

We all swung around to see Hansen in his car, smoke billowing out of the driver's window.

"He's going to kill me!" she exclaimed. "You need to help me."

Heidi was known for her psychotic episodes, so nobody really took her seriously. Einar wasn't aware of her mental state, although he obviously knew about her attack on Aggie last year, but I think he was starting to understand what she was really like. He returned to the reception area, pulling the door shut, just to be safe.

She made a dash for it and Hansen pulled out in front of a bus, trying to get to her. We watched him for a couple of minutes as he tried to manoeuvre a U-turn, which failed completely.

"Are you alright, baby?" Thor asked, concern on his face.

I nodded. "She thinks that Hansen is going to kill her. She says that he killed Aggie."

He shook his head in disbelief. "You believe her?" he asked.

"I'm not sure, I don't think so. It was her who came out of the building last that day. She came out of the bathroom. She had been physical with Aggie before."

He nodded. "Well, I'll stay by your side to keep you safe," he told me.

I sure as hell didn't want that! "N…no, we don't need to do that. She'll have still won if she takes my freedom away," I declined delicately.

"I'd rather you have limited freedom than no life," he explained.

"Your work has you starting as I finish work though," I protested.

"I'll quit my job if necessary!"

"YOU WILL NOT!" I responded firmly.

"Well, we'll discuss it over the weekend," he concluded. "Now, let's get you home. I've made a booking at a nice restaurant for tonight."

"Why?"

"For a special treat for you," he smiled.

"But it's my girl's…"

"It's my day off though. We've not seen much of you recently. I'm sure they'll understand."

He held his hand out and squeezed mine tightly until we reached the flat. He pulled my bag off my arm and placed it on the breakfast bar.

"You'll need fancy clothes," he told me.

His hand remained on my bag. I prised it away from him.

"Are you ok?" he asked.

"Yeah, it was just a shock. I'll probably listen to music on my phone to calm me down."

He nodded and I entered the bathroom. I had no friends that I could talk to about this, but didn't want him to have access to my bag! Luckily, most of my important things were stored at the gym in my locker, but I wasn't 100% sure that there was nothing in my bag that could cause an issue. My going-out clothes were at the gym, too, as was my makeup bag. There were a couple of bits still here in case I couldn't make it to the gym before work; just a little lip gloss and mascara – that would have to do.

I found something light to wear which wasn't too shabby. I blow-dried my hair, so it looked slightly better and decided that was as good as it was going to get. I returned to the kitchen.

"We don't have much food in the place, do we?" he commented. "We'll have to nip to the supermarket tomorrow."

'NOPE NOPE NOPE!', I thought to myself. "We are not upheaving our entire lives just because of one crazy woman!" I insisted. I so didn't need him staying off work this weekend! "I very much doubt that she'll even attempt to contact me again. Hansen will have a very tight rein on her!"

"Just for a couple of weeks, then," he suggested.

"NO!" I said firmly, hugging him. "I will be fine!"

"Maybe I could…"

"STOP! If you stop work, change work or anything similar, then she would have won. Mr Olsen is on the reception desk now at the office, so she won't be able to get me there. I bet he'd give me a lift home if I feel I need it. Let's not become her victim, in any way!"

He nodded, took my hand and led me out to a waiting taxi. It was a short journey to… Apparatjik! The posh restaurant that Erik worked at.

"Oh, we can't eat here," I protested.

"Why?" he asked, with a glint in his eye.

"It's so expensive here, Thor, we can't…"

"How would you know?"

"Mamma took me, last year I think it was," I replied, not lying.

"Don't worry," he smiled. "I've been saving."

'Saving the rent money!' I thought to myself.

We walked to the entrance, and Thor spoke to the greeter. I tried to retrieve my phone to send Erik a text, but Thor was too closely guarded to me. He raised his eyebrows.

"Just switching my phone off. Can you imagine how uncouth that would be, to have a phone ringing in a place like this?!" I laughed forcibly.

We sat at a small table and the waiter brought the menu over to us. It wasn't Erik, luckily, but I did keep my eyes panning around for him. I felt so sad. I didn't want him to witness this.

"Any idea what you would like?" Thor asked me.

I shook my head. I'd remembered from last time how intricate the menu was. Nothing was making sense to me with my head screaming for release; literal release.

"We're still perusing the menu at present," Thor spoke fancily. "We'll start with some champagne."

I stared at him blankly. We couldn't afford champagne from a regular shop, let alone a Michelin star restaurant! I felt panic rising inside me.

"We can't afford this, Thor!" I whispered to him.

He put his finger to his lips. "Don't worry, sweetie."

The waiter brought out the bottle of champagne, and opened it, making me jump. He poured it into the glasses. "Leave the bottle," Thor insisted.

I was mentally working out how much the bottle was. I ordered something that looked cheap for my main course, skipping the starter. Thor chose to have a starter, of course, so I was at a loose end.

The restaurant started filling up with more customers. I had no appetite at all now. I picked at my main course, which wasn't particularly nice anyway. Thor gestured to a waiter to come and fill our glasses for us. It was Erik.

"We...we can fill our glasses up ourselves," I whispered to him, struggling to breathe.

"These waiters earn shit loads, Line, they should earn their money! Fill 'em up, *Erika!*"

I looked at my glass, not wanting to look at Erik, my face burning. Thor nodded to him and stood up, giving me the opportunity to look at Erik to mouth my apologies, until I realised that Thor was kneeling next to me. I couldn't see what he was doing, until he loudly asked me to marry him. He opened a small box which contained the most vulgar diamond and ruby ring that I had ever seen. My heart dropped into my stomach, and I stood up.

Forgetting that we were in a fancy restaurant, I said, "No. Not ever. I have no intention of marrying you – EVER. I don't even want to live with you. I'm moving to a new apartment soon, and you're not even coming with me. What part of that do you *not* understand??!"

"Why would you humiliate me like this? We're in this fantastic restaurant, and I've done this grand gesture, and you show me up by saying no?!" he ranted back at me.

"What gave you the impression that I wanted any of this?"

"All girls want this," he replied.

"NO! We don't. Have you not noticed that I've been changing my whole sleeping pattern to avoid you?"

"Excuse me, sir, madam, could you please continue this elsewhere? Here is the bill, and we'll call you a taxi if you want?"

Thor swung round to be face-to-face with the manager of the restaurant.

"NO! I don't want you to call me a taxi!" He swiped his hand across the table and all of the glassware, and the champagne bottle flew across the table and onto the floor. He promptly stormed off and left me.

Tears flooded my eyes, and I just slumped to the floor. Erik was with me in a second, hugging me tightly. "Let me help you up, Line," he suggested.

"I'm so sorry, Erik, I had no idea. I'm sorry if I've got you into trouble."

"Shhh," he soothed me.

He helped me up and took me to the manager's office. I cried for what seemed like an eternity, and he just held me in his arms.

"I managed to get myself a new apartment this week and I'm moving in tomorrow. He knows nothing about it – as far as I'm aware," I explained to him.

"Why didn't you talk to me about it?" he asked.

"I haven't been able to tell anyone, I've just done it all by myself."

He held me again.

"I…I have some money for this – I assume he didn't pay?" I asked, apologetically.

"No, I don't think so."

"Ok…" I regained my composure, "I have some in my…locker… at the gym…" I said between sobs.

"I'll see if I can speak to the manager, just give me a few minutes."

He sat me on a comfy chair and called the manager over. They stood in a corner whispering, then Erik returned to me again.

"It's all sorted. He's going to take it out of my wages for the week," he smiled at me, brushing my hair away from my face, some of which was stuck to the tears.

"I...I will pay you back in a bit, I'll j...just go to the gym on my way home..."

"Isn't it my turn anyway? You bought the last refreshments!" he laughed.

"There's a big difference between a hot chocolate and a three-course meal at Apparatjik's!"

"I get paid more than enough, apparently," he smirked.

"I'm so sorry, I had no idea he was taking me here. I didn't even know he had booked anything till I finished work!"

"Another Friday of no girls' night out, eh? Coincidence?"

"He's been playing me, hasn't he?"

Erik shrugged. "Did you want me to come back to the flat with you, in case he's still raging?"

"No, but thanks. He'll rage more if you're there than if you weren't."

"Is there anywhere else you could stay tonight?" he asked.

"Only the new apartment," I replied. "There are some bits there, that the landlord has supplied. Getting there could be an issue, but I'll play it by ear."

"If you need anything, just call or text me. The manager will let me go early if I need to. He's seen Thor's rage already, so knows that you may need help."

"Ok," I nodded.

"The taxi is here," the greeter popped his head around the door.

"Anything…" Erik whispered in my ear.

I squeezed his hand and nodded, keeping my head down as I walked to the car.

Back at the flat, I was apprehensive to go inside. I inhaled deeply and walked up the stairs.

"Not staying with your boyfriend, then?" the outburst began immediately.

"Don't put this on him," I replied angrily. "It was YOU who decided we should eat there, when you knew he worked there. Who do you think is going to pay for all that?"

"I couldn't care less," he shouted, walking towards the bags of the clothes and soft furnishings that I'd packed, and slashed them with a kitchen knife that he had in his hand.

All of my clothes were then strewn across the flat.

"It's on the news!" Kristian announced.

"What?" I replied, confused by this. Had someone filmed our 'issue' at the restaurant?

"YOU AREN'T MOVING ANYWHERE!" he bellowed, grabbing my shoulders and bringing my attention back to him.

"Oh yes I am!" I replied, a few decibels lower than him.

I pushed away from him and made it to the bathroom, slamming the door. I listened through the door to see if I could hear what else he was doing. I could hear things smashing, so I returned to the kitchen to find him smashing all of my mugs, including one which my parents had bought me for my 18th.

"You'll have nothing to take with you, then!"

He started pulling out all the plates and bowls and smashing them on the floor too.

"It's on the news, guys, she's dead!"

"What?" I replied. "Who is?"

"Mrs Hansen!"

"What?" I repeated.

Thor stopped what he was doing and walked over to the TV. "Found stabbed to death in an alleyway close to your work!" he turned to face me.

Kristian turned the volume up on the TV so we could all hear it.

"...stabbed in the chest and left close to her husband's office at Olsen Business Services. This comes just a few short months after the building's receptionist, Agnes Johnsen was murdered in the same way, in the same location..."

I didn't know quite what to do. I was dumbstruck. She was right, and it must have been Hansen!

Chapter 25 – Make It Soon

I barely slept that night. When I did wake up fully, I found that the boys hadn't gone to work.

"We are keeping you safe!" Thor announced. "You were only threatened last night."

"I wasn't threatened, she was warning me."

"Either way, I'm not leaving you alone in the flat. He knows where you live, doesn't he?"

I nodded. Quite frankly, I thought I'd rather die than be held hostage by the Valles. Kris was bouncing around the flat like a maniac.

"He could have gone, couldn't he?!" I nodded at Kristian.

Thor shrugged. "Can't hurt to have him around."

The TV was blaring on the news 24 channel, Kris thriving from it. I shook my head and went for a shower. What was I going to do? How long would it be before they returned to work? How long would I be stuck in this flat for? What if Hansen was going to kill me?

I busied myself with repacking all of the items that Thor had unbagged last night. I stored each one in my closet for now. Thor was glued to the TV with his brother. I managed to have a text conversation with Erik, who was doubly worried about my safety. He initially assumed that Thor had killed Heidi, until it was discovered that she had died before he'd left the restaurant.

'I just need to get out of here. I need to go to Hansen's place to check for clues!' I text him.

'No, you can't risk it. He's a suspect and she said you were next!'.

'There are photos that he's taken of me!'.

'Not important. Police will deal with that.'

'I can't just live in fear forever. I need to find out if he's after me or not!'.

'There'll be police crawling all over the place rn. Just leave it'.

I wasn't going to leave it, but put it on the back burner for now. My most important task for now was how to get my stuff to the new apartment. I had managed to fit everything into the closet, although the doors wouldn't shut completely. It would have to be a very quick, frantic move rather than having the luxury of both boys being at work. I was good at adapting to new predicaments, and would have to do just that now.

~

I had paced like a caged tiger all day. The boys had played their video games for most of the time, and I even thought about making a run for it while they were distracted. There was no coffee to keep me awake and alert, so instead I did the opposite – I took a couple of my sedatives with half a bottle of wine and slept for the rest of the day.

I woke up around 5 a.m. and both the boys were asleep. I started to quietly pull out the clothes and soft furnishing bags, stacking them by the front door. Seeing that I hadn't disturbed either brother, I stood outside the front door to call a taxi, which would be there in just a few minutes. I took a deep breath and returned indoors. There was still no movement. In no time, I received a text message to say that the taxi had arrived, and I jumped into action, frantically throwing the bags down the stairs one after the other. Once they were all downstairs, I loaded the bags into the taxi, apologising to the driver. He smiled at me and helped me put some on the front seat too.

We were soon on our way and finally I knew I was safe. I asked the driver if he could make sure that if anyone contacted him for my destination, he wouldn't tell them. Unless it was the police, of course! He understood the situation.

The taxi arrived at the new apartment and the driver got out and helped me unload the bags, ensuring I was safely inside the building before he drove away. I tipped him quite a bit on the OsloTaxi app once I, and my bags reached my apartment.

I was free!

I threw all of the bags into the bedroom for now. If it hadn't been for the lack of toiletries, I would have had a shower, but I slowly walked round the entire apartment, mentally noting down what I needed for each room. In the kitchen, I found a lovely little fridge freezer, and in the fridge there was some milk. A hamper was gift-wrapped and placed on the counter, full of food and drink items, like coffee, tea, sugar, fruit, biscuits and a kettle. A handwritten note read: 'Welcome to your new home Line - Einar'.

It had seemed like ages since I had consumed coffee, so that was my first priority. I sat on my new sofa, a very clean light-grey one, closed my eyes and breathed. Perfect!

I munched on biscuits and slurped on freedom coffee, before happily unpacking all of my clothes and hanging them in *my* wardrobe -MY wardrobe! I put clean sheets onto *my* new bed, a double bed provided by Einar. Cushions were placed on the sofa, although the covers didn't really match it. Once the curtains were up, and a blanket draped on the sofa, it looked much better. Very boho!

I felt hungry for the first time in days, but didn't have anything there except for the fruit. Normally that would have sufficed, but I had this overwhelming need for food. I looked at the time on my phone. It was a decent time now, so could pop out to get some groceries. Slightly concerned about Hansen, I decided to get a taxi to a supermarket and then another to come home again. I still had the 5,000 kroner from the Valles, and fully intended to keep it. I checked how much room was in the freezer and opened a few cupboards too. There was plenty of space for at least a week's food.

It was the same driver who had helped me earlier, and he enquired if I was ok. I smiled and assured him that I was great. The walk around the supermarket was euphoric. I could buy what I wanted, not having to consider the brothers. I received a few phone calls as I strolled the aisles; it was Thor. I of course ignored it and managed a few more aisles before Pappa called me.

"Hi, Pappa," I answered swiftly.

"How are you, Bumblebee?"

"I'm good thanks."

"So, I've had Thor just call me…"

"So sorry. I meant to contact you before he could, but I didn't get the chance."

"He says you have gone missing."

I laughed. "No, I moved out of the flat."

"Ok...? Why?"

"Just gave up, I guess. They were taking me for a mug and just trashing the place. I had eventually got them to make an effort and pay some money towards the expenses. They paid for one week in the last six. It got me to the point where I just didn't want to be there anymore."

"But you are ok?"

"Yes," I replied. "I'm just out shopping for some food. Can I call you back when I'm back home?"

"Of course. Glad I got to speak to you rather than just text messages!"

I concluded my grocery shopping, and an OsloTaxi driver dropped me off outside my new home. This driver wasn't the same guy this time, and he drove off as soon as all my groceries were out of his vehicle. Luckily there was a lift, as these bags were much heavier than the soft items from the old flat. I made a mental note to revert to daily shops in future, as this was quite tricky.

I called Pappa back as I put away the groceries.

"So you know about the murder then?" I started.

"I heard there was a murder in the city. Were you connected to it then?"

"It's my old boss' wife who was murdered. It was just behind the office, and she was killed in the same way as Aggie."

"So there could be a connection between them?"

"Yeah, I think so. This victim, Heidi, was the one who I thought had killed Aggie. Heidi confronted me on Friday afternoon, just before she was murdered, and also came Aggie's funeral and told me that she thought her husband had done it, and that she was next. Last night she said that she feared for her life and that I'd be next on the list."

"WOW. Well, I guess it makes more sense that Thor was worried about you."

"I had been planning to leave for a few weeks, but only got this place a few days ago. I had packed most of my stuff, with the plan to move this weekend, and then, because of the murder he decided to stay off work yesterday and I was worried that I'd never get out. He slashed all the bags I had packed and threw everything around the flat."

"You didn't need to rush though, did you?"

"I wanted to be out of there weeks ago, and everything else just fell into place until Friday. I plan to go there about a week before the tenancy ends to clean it as much as I can. I've told Thor when he needs to be out by."

"Well, I'll make sure to come and help…"

"Pappa, you can't come all this way to just help me clean the flat…"

"It's not just the cleaning, it's being a backup in case Thor and his brother cause issues."

"I'll be fi…"

"Stop arguing with me, missy!"

I laughed. "It's a long way for…"

"Are you still arguing?"

"No, sir!"

"Correct!"

"Please, please make sure that no one tells any of the Valles where I am."

"Naturally. Send me your address."

"Yep, will do."

Next, I text a message to Erik, to let him know that I'd successfully moved and was safe. I knew he would be getting ready for work, if not already there.

I made myself a little lunch – salmon and cream cheese wraps. They were amazing. 'I shall call them freedom wraps', I thought to myself. I ensured that I washed up all of the pots that I used as soon as I'd finished using them. Obviously it's the logical thing to do, but things had been a little lax back at the flat. *Start as you mean to go on*, I think Mamma's phrase was.

I found myself at a loose end by the afternoon. I remembered that Marit had asked for some help converting the coffee shop, so I text her to see if she still needed me. I made a coffee while I waited for her response. The whole apartment had been cleaned by Einar, or one of his 'guys', but I still gave it a second clean. Food was all stored where it needed to be. I made a note on my phone to get more crockery. I was still devastated about all the mugs that Thor had broken, but I had to move on. I could nip into a couple of shops after work tomorrow.

Finally, at around 3.30 p.m., Marit replied.

'Wd lv it if u cd pop rnd, if ur still free?''

I was pleased to read this. 'Be there asap! Do u need anything bringing?''

I grabbed my bag and the new home keys, then paused. 'How am I going to get there?'. I knew that public transport was available in this new area, but I wasn't sure where or when, especially on a Sunday! I thought for a second – it'd have to be a taxi. I ordered one and it was with me within a couple of minutes.

It was the same driver that helped me to leave Thor. He smiled at me.

"You are a busy lady!" he laughed.

"So are you...well... man! You work long hours!"

"Pays the bills, eh?!"

I nodded, "Sure does. As much as I love getting taxis everywhere, is there a quick, safe way to get to the centre from here?"

"No, you MUST get taxis!" he laughed. "There should be timetables for routes at the stations. Or online, I guess."

"It's not too far. Is it walkable, do you think? I've never really been to this area, so it is a little unfamiliar for me."

"It's quite a way to walk, but doable. Be careful though, there's been a couple of murders near where you are going this time."

I nodded. "Yeah, I'm more than aware of them. I found the first one, and had only just talked to the one from Friday before she was murdered. She even told me that I could be next! Hence why I'm getting taxis!"

"WOW!" He exclaimed. "That must have been terrible. Are the police not protecting you?"

I thought for a few seconds. "I really don't know. I haven't spoken to them..." I had been so wrapped up in leaving Thor that I had barely thought about it. "I'll have to pop in tomorrow."

We arrived at the coffee shop, and I thanked him. I got out and he waited until I was safely in the premises before leaving. I sent him a tip on the OsloTaxi app.

"Oooh, how posh are you, Line! Marit must be paying you too much if you can afford that extravagance!" Frøya announced, as she opened the door for me.

"There's a murderer around!" I replied, pulling a face. "I see that boss lady roped you into this too then!" I laughed.

"How are you doing, Line?" Marit appeared, with concern all over her face.

"I'm ok," I replied. "What do you know?"

This intrigued her further. "That there was another murder just behind the office building, identical to Aggie's."

"Ok," I nodded.

"Is there more to it then?" she pressed further.

I nodded again, taking a seat at a table. Marit sat down with me and Frøya brought us all coffees.

"The woman who was murdered was Heidi Hansen, my ex-boss' wife."

Frøya gasped.

"A matter of minutes before she was murdered, she approached me, outside the office building, and she was really distressed. As well as Friday, she had told me the same at Aggie's funeral; she said that it was Kenneth Hansen, her husband who killed Aggie, and she thought that he would kill her next."

There was silence for a minute or so as they processed the information.

"So you had been working for a potential murderer? A serial killer?" Frøya finally deduced.

"Well, she also said that he would come after me after this. It's no secret that he didn't like me."

"OH MY GOD! What did the police say?" Marit asked.

"I haven't even spoken to them. I've had a very eventful weekend! It's only just sinking in now, I think."

"Well, get down to the station, or at least give them a call. Did you want me to drive you to and from work if they don't provide any security?"

"Well, that's the 'eventful stuff that happened' information..."

I explained everything that had happened, and they were both stunned.

"Why didn't you tell me, Line?" Marit asked.

"I didn't tell anyone. Although there are people in my life that I fully trust, including you, Marit, I just had to be so careful."

"So how are you going to get to work and back? Do you need some time off work?"

"NO! MOST DEFINITELY NOT!" I said emphatically. "It'll have to be taxis for now."

"But that'll be so expensive though," Frøya said.

I nodded. "I know, but I love my job," I smiled at Marit, "and I would go stir crazy at home all the time!"

"It's just so expensive though!" Frøya repeated.

I nodded and drained my coffee cup. "C'mon, let's get this shop sorted!"

Heidi Hansen

Chapter 26 – The End of the Affair

I woke up before my alarm the next morning, still in a state of euphoria. The rest of yesterday afternoon had been fun, we all worked great together converting the shop. I was excited to get to work.

I received a text at 05:12 from Marit, saying that she was going to pick me up and take me to work. I tried to protest but she was having none of it. Normally I would have been at the gym right now, but my vulnerability had set in.

Marit had arranged to take me to the police station after we'd finished with the shop, and she even sat in the waiting area for me. A police officer had taken my statement about both incidents with Heidi.

The officer couldn't offer any kind of protection – it wasn't a dramatic movie with resources like witness protection! She did give words of advice, such as being aware of my surroundings, don't go down alleyways, stay in busy areas. I pointed out that both murders were just seconds away from busy areas. Not to mention that they were seconds away from my old, and new, workplaces.

I asked about Hansen. She said he couldn't confirm any lines of enquiry, or tell people about suspects. Looking at it, there was no sign of a quick resolution, although I was assured that they would look into it. Surely this would just aggravate him more? I had left the station feeling no safer.

~

As I showered for work this morning, I contemplated getting a bike, but realised that he could easily just grab and stab without anyone knowing that it would happen. He could knock me off it, and even reverse over me. My mind was clearly working overtime, but this was appeased with Marit's intention to collect me on her way to work. I checked my phone, it was just after 5 a.m. I still had time for a quick coffee. I sat in my living room, looking out of the window to check for Marit's arrival. When I spotted her car, I waved and dashed into the kitchen to turn the coffee pot off and wash my cup.

This was the first day for the new layout, following my ideas for the shop's progress, and I felt really proud of it. I was a little nervous when I realised that Marit parked her car in the car park behind the shops, as it was where Heidi was murdered. It had been re-opened to the public, but there was still the odd bit of police tape flapping around in the breeze. I sat in my seat a few seconds longer than Marit, as I processed this little bit of information.

"Breathe," Marit told me when she saw my hesitation.

I had felt my anxiety levels rising, but the breathing helped to calm me down. There was a back entrance to the coffee shop, and once we stepped in, Marit over-exaggerated the locking of the door for my peace of mind.

"We usually keep it unlocked, for rubbish disposal and staff breaks, but it will be unlocked when necessary and then re-locked again. I will be letting Frøya know when she comes in too."

"I don't want to imprison anyone…"

"We want to make sure you are safe. That takes priority."

I nodded and smiled weakly. We entered the main shop and admired our work. There was a massive sign in the front window, indicating which door a customer would be best to queue at. There were smaller signs either side of the doors to reinforce the choice. The café was already cleaned, I had given it a thorough scrub yesterday, so I just gave it a quick 'once-over' for peace of mind.

Each table had one of the mason jars with either coffee beans or fruity potpourri in, with a table number stuck on it. I had drawn out a rough floorplan so that I knew which table was which, until I got used to it. There were menus on each table, with stickers on, indicating that they could approach the counter or download the app.

As soon as Marit had finished cleaning the coffee machine, she brought me a cup of the freshly-brewed black liquid.

"Are you ok to work today?" she asked.

"Can't wait," I replied. "I'm really excited!"

Frøya arrived, ready for her shift. She joined us at the table.

"Right, so the plan is, you and Frøya work your 'stations', or 'areas' I suppose. I'll be the 'runner', because then I can stay alert that both of you are ok, plus make any sandwiches not currently stocked, as normal."

"Have you had to change everything because of me?" I asked.

"What do you mean?" she frowned.

"You 'staying alert'?"

"Well, I will, of course be keeping a look out for various threats. But that's my job as boss lady, whether your life is in danger or not." I sighed. "It's not a biggie," she smiled reassuringly. "Are we ready to open?" she asked.

I nodded and she opened both doors. Frøya and I applauded and cheered.

"We should have had some ribbon for you to cut with giant scissors," I laughed, after I had recorded this monumentous day for her on my phone.

We had decided that the 'eating in' customers choose their own seating, as it was before the changes. It was all a trial, which could be tweaked as necessary. App orders would appear on the 'eat-in' section of the till, which update on Marit's phone as soon as the order was placed. I could also use the 'eat-in' section till to take orders.

The first few customers filtered in, and I could see customers on Frøya's side too. We caught sight of each other and grinned. I felt excited as I waited patiently at the counter. I saw a couple of people looking at their phones, and an elderly gentleman came to the counter to order.

"I don't understand all these apps," he explained.

I smiled. "We'll be controlling things with our minds in no time," I joked with him.

I took his order and let him know that we'd bring everything to him. The queues flowed nicely and Marit buzzed around behind the counter like a little bee. The takeaway customers were served quicker because the eating in customers weren't in their queue, just as I had thought and was why I had suggested it. It still seemed busy for as long as usual. It calmed down at the usual time, around my lunch break. I was just choosing my food when Einar arrived.

"Hello, Mr Olsen," I greeted him. "Are you eating in today?"

"Good morning, Miss Larsen," he replied, smiling. "Unfortunately, no. I have locked the doors briefly so that I can come to collect you. I figured that you would be a little reluctant to walk the short distance alone, but I enjoy your company and it's not going to be healthy to stay indoors all the time."

"Oh, thank you, Mr Olsen."

I quickly gathered up all of my lunch items and my bag and followed him back to the office building, very apprehensive that Hansen would pop out of nowhere.

Safely inside the office, Einar sat me in a chair behind the counter. "This little space just here is a blind spot for people at the front of the building. Mr Hansen no longer has an office here, so has no need to come by. I will escort you back to the café every day, if you so choose. I know it's still indoors, for now, but at least it is a different environment."

I nodded. "It's good to get out. Marit collected me from the apartment this morning, on her way to work. I'm going to look into public transport on my break, I hope you don't mind. Normally I'd walk, and I did contemplate getting a bike, but I don't feel that it is safe enough right now. I was using taxis yesterday, and obviously that won't do long term. Hopefully, Mr Hansen will be charged and not have bail, very soon!"

"That would be great," Einar smiled, "If it was him, of course."

"You don't think it was?" I questioned.

"As long as they get whoever committed these heinous murders, I really don't mind. Until they are caught, you aren't living your life completely."

I nodded. "I've already had to stop going to the gym at the moment."

"Public transport is pretty good in Oslo, to be honest," Einar explained. "You can more or less get from the apartment to here."

"I'm more worried about times, to be honest. I start work at 6 a.m."

"They run at that time."

I smiled and sighed with relief, and within a few clicks and a couple of minutes I had managed to purchase a weekly ticket, on the 'Ruter' app. We spent the rest of the time chatting about my apartment and the area I now lived in. I at least had some invisibility to ensure that Hansen kept his distance – for now.

I returned to the café after my break to find Marit standing at the door waiting for me.

"Oh no, what's happened?" I felt panicky.

A huge grin spread across her face. "We've run out of bread! We have had so many customers that we've run. out. of. food!!" she explained breathlessly. "I have to pop out and get some more!"

"You should have texted me, I could have got some."

"I'm not having you running around town right now."

"Well, I could have come back earlier."

"Maybe, but I'd better go now!"

She dashed out of the door, and I went to the staff area to put my bag into my locker, before grabbing the cleaning equipment to sort out the customer area. Marit arrived back in no time and disappeared into the kitchen to make up some orders. She had prioritised the takeaway customers, so that queue was almost empty now, and the indoor customers were happy with their beverages. She returned with five plates of sandwiches, and I took a few out of her hands and served the customers.

In no time, it was the end of my workday. I was desperate to have a nosey around the shops, but knew that it may not be safe enough. Einar arrived to escort me to the office building, and I handed him his food order.

"I won't be able to stay till you lock up for a while, I want to vary my routine to avoid any issues." Einar nodded. "I'm going to go to the gym shortly. I've really missed the place, and it's only been a few days!"

"Sounds fabulous, maybe I should join!" Einar laughed.

I left after about half an hour, and hopped on a bus that would take me to my destination. I sat in the gym lounge, feeling slightly less nervous about my safety. As I consumed coffee I tapped away at my phone, to look for transport home and to see if there were any stores near my new home. There were quite a lot right on my doorstep, not literally of course. I did also find that it was quite cycle-friendly with lots of cycle lanes, and even hire bikes; this was definitely a route I wanted to go by. Apparently, I'd be able to cycle to work within 15 minutes. I remembered that there was an 'Oslo Bysykkel' station just outside the clothes shop that was a couple of doors down from the café, in the opposite direction to the office building. Perfect! I made a mental note to observe the route to work and back over the next couple of days.

After a great workout, I showered and changed, and dragged everything out of my locker to be washed. I tucked the money envelope securely amongst my dry clothes and headed for the bus.

Heidi Hansen

<u>Chapter 27 – Don't Do Me Any Favours</u>

Public transport went smoothly, and I had successfully made it home last night and to work this morning. Marit greeted me at the bus stop, to ensure that I arrived from the bus stop to the café front door safely. There was a coffee on the staff area table by the time I had hung my bags up.

"Yesterday was so amazing here, Line. I've never known it to be so busy!" Marit started.

"I was rushed off my feet," I nodded.

"I hope I'm not on the wrong track, but I don't think we need a two-month appraisal. You have been absolutely amazing. Your fresh ideas and hard work have been impeccable! If you still want to spend the rest of the probation deciding if you want to stay here or not, then that is fine."

"You want me to stay?" I asked.

"Yes, if you want to stay?"

I nodded. "Of course. I've enjoyed these last few weeks more than nearly a year with Hansen!"

"I'm so glad. I'm so happy you were brave to give it a try. I will do some paperwork, and then I'm going to give you a pay rise from Sunday."

"From Sunday?" I replied.

She nodded, "Yes, last Sunday. Despite dealing with a relationship breakup, the murder of someone you knew very well and moving home, you still came in to help us convert the shop!"

I smiled. "It helped me no end!"

"Good!" Marit beamed, standing up to clean the coffee machine.

I followed her, collecting the cleaning products to make a start on the customer area. I hated the fact that I left before the café closed and couldn't have the peace of mind that it was cleaned well enough, although I'm sure that the other girl does it just fine. Once I had centred all of the mason jars, I ventured over to the 'takeaway' section and gave the floor a thorough sweep and mop. Afterwards, I stood for a moment to admire this section that I hadn't spent much time in since the revamp. It looked great, with a couple of chairs for customers waiting for their custom orders to the side of the doors.

Marit joined me shortly. "Ready to open?" she asked.

"Yep!" I responded, returning to the staff area to store the cleaning items.

She opened both doors and people started filtering in. Yesterday, I'd found that standing near the till was encouraging them to assume I wanted them to come to me, so I perched on a stool just a little way back from the counter. Several tables were filled instantly, and all seemed to be on their phones sorting out the app. I sat with one lady who couldn't work out how to do it, and I helped her to add it, showing her how to order.

Throughout the morning, the place was buzzing with activity. Marit had to remind me to have my break. When I disappeared into the staff area to get my bag, she approached me. "I forgot to ask, did you sort your sedatives out?" she asked discreetly.

"Well, I'm not taking them anymore, but haven't been to see the doctor to confirm this."

"I can give you a little time off to go and see them if you need to. It looks like I may need you to be trained on the machines. It's just so busy," she beamed breathlessly.

"I'll call on my break, to make an appointment," I nodded.

Marit passed me the two coffees for me to take to Olsen's, and I turned around and Einar was waiting by the door for me, to escort me safely. He nodded to greet me, and I smiled back at him.

"How did you get on with the buses?" he asked, as we walked the short distance between properties.

"Easy peasy!" I replied.

He held the door open for me, and I walked over to my new seat behind the desk. He presented me with two pastries. "I came to the café earlier," he explained, "the new layout looks great. I must admit, I have attempted to come in before, and was put off by the queues. Today, I was in and out in around a minute."

"I'll let Marit know the positive feedback," I smiled, flaky pastry dropping from my mouth.

"It's very difficult to eat these pastries with dignity!" Einar laughed, as he cut his up into tiny pieces.

"You won't even taste it!" I laughed.

"It's ideal for when you need to look professional, though," he explained, indicating someone approaching the desk.

I leaned forward. "Can I make a quick call please?" I requested.

He nodded toward the back office. I nipped in and called the doctor who had prescribed my sedatives. The earliest I could get an appointment for was next Monday. I decided to continue to not take them, seeing as there didn't seem to be any withdrawal symptoms. I sat on the comfortable chair at the desk. There were two piles of folders on the desk, with names on. I spotted one for

Hansen and discreetly lifted the corner of the card folder and spotted his address.

I heard Einar's chair squeak as he stood up, so I quickly returned the folder and turned away from the desk. I put my phone back in my bag and stood up.

"Another two clients have cancelled their tenancies," he shook his head.

"Oh no!" I exclaimed, regaining my composure. "That's not good!"

"Another murder right next to the building, I don't blame them!" he sighed.

"Will it pick up for you, do you think?" I asked.

"No, I don't think so," he replied. "There's only about five clients left."

"How many offices are there?" I enquired.

"Fifteen," he replied. "I could relocate the offices to another building, but the chances of me being able to sell this place... not good!"

I shook my head. It wasn't fair to him, it was purely unlucky circumstances.

Another tenant approached the desk just as I was about to leave. I touched him on the shoulder and smiled empathically. "I can make my own way back," I whispered and left him to it.

As I left the building, my phone rang. I stood against the wall, so as to not get in anyone's way, to retrieve it from my bag. It was the doctor, and it had taken me too long as it was a missed call. I waited to see if the caller would leave a voicemail, and I became aware of someone standing next to me. Einar must have decided to escort me home after all, I thought as I looked up. It was Hansen.

I gasped, and I could feel my heart rate increase. Panic enveloped me. I held my breath and looked round to see if there was anyone who could help. My mouth went dry, and I tried to escape.

"Larsen, calm down!" he hissed in my ear, grabbing me by my elbow. "No one is stupid enough to hurt someone with all of these people around!"

I wasn't convinced; maybe it was *too* busy for anyone to notice.

"Look, Larsen, I know you don't like me, and I know that I've never really liked you, but listen. I never killed Mrs Johnsen, or my wife. That I will swear to. I have no intention of hurting you either."

I felt myself getting lightheaded and worried that I was going to pass out. "You need to watch your step and stay aware of your surroundings, just in case!"

I felt my legs give way beneath me, and Einar was with me in two strides, holding me up. "Are you ok, Line?" he probed.

Hansen was nowhere in sight. I tried to speak, but couldn't.

"Come back to the office," he suggested.

"No!" I insisted. "That's where he got Aggie!"

Einar nodded. "I heard him threaten you, I was just going to take you in so I could call the police.

I steadied myself against him and the wall, thanking him. He helped me to the café instead.

"Don't make a scene," I whispered as we got to the door. "I don't want to panic any of the customers."

He laughed gently. "Come on, then."

I managed to walk by myself, and headed straight for the staff area, before sliding to the ground and bursting into tears.

Marit was with me in seconds. "Mr Olsen said that you had seen Hansen?"

I nodded my head. "He said... he..."

"Breathe, Line," Marit comforted.

"The customers..." I exclaimed, "don't lose any customers."

"Don't worry about that, Line, Frøya can handle that. It's quieter now."

"I feel sick," I announced, getting up to go to the bathroom just in time.

When I returned, she sat me onto a chair and brought me some water.

"I'm so sorry," I said, trying to breathe slower.

"Shush!" Marit replied.

"It was just so close to... close to where..."

"Take your time," she replied, pushing my hair away from my sweaty forehead.

There was a knock at the back door and I literally jumped to my feet.

"It's ok, Line, it'll be the police. I think Mr Olsen asked them to come to the back so it doesn't affect customers," she explained, walking to the door.

"What if it's Hansen, he'll get you!" I panicked.

She stood at the door, thinking about her next move. "There's a window in the stockroom," she said, entering the room. "The windows have bars on them, for safety."

She returned to the back door. "It's definitely the police," she announced, opening the door.

I wasn't sure if Marit had seen Hansen before. How did I know for sure that it was the real police and not him pretending? I stood up, holding the wooden sweeping brush handle, ready to strike or run.

"Miss Larsen?" one of the men approached me. "I'm here about a threat that was made to you?"

The other one, a tall, dark-haired younger man, stood by the door and spoke to Marit. My officer definitely wasn't Hansen, but I thoroughly checked his ID before I put the brush down. I sat back down on the chair and sipped the water. He said his name, but my brain didn't process the information. He took as much information from me that I could provide, and said that there was enough to take Hansen in for questioning. I asked if he could let me know when Hansen was in, and out, of the station, so that I knew when it was safe to go home. He nodded and gave me his card.

"If you think of anything, or need anything, here's my office number and my mobile number."

"Thanks," I replied, holding his card with clammy hands.

They both left and Marit returned to the table.

"How are you?" she asked, concern on her face.

"This was just a small encounter. Just a small taste of what that man is really like," I replied, shaking my head. "That poor wife of his. It must have been awful."

'I must continue to have Heidi Hansen as my client!', I decided, 'for justice!'.

<u>Chapter 28 – Summer Rain</u>

I must have sat in that chair for hours, as it was Marit who had approached me and offered to drive me home.

"No, no, you have work..." I'd protested.

"Darling, the café is shut now," she had explained.

I'd still felt very shaky and nauseous. She had walked close to me, as we made the short journey to her car, and had helped me into the front seat. The ride home was quick, and Marit was thorough with the checking of the area before she escorted me to the building. She had insisted on coming up to my apartment with me.

"Let me make you a drink?" she had suggested.

I'd had a nasty taste in my mouth, but had shook my head. "I think I just want to brush my teeth and go to bed," I'd replied.

"No problem," she had smiled. "Do you need anything before I go?" she'd offered.

I'd shook my head and attempted to smile back.

"Take tomorrow off work, and Thursday, if necessary. I'll check in with you tomorrow. Let me know if you need anything."

~

I was woken the next morning by a phone call. It was an unknown number, but I still answered it.

"Hi, Miss Larsen, it's Overkonstabel Stefan Jakobsen, from Oslo Police."

"Hi?" I replied croakily, clearing my throat.

"Just an update, Line…may I call you Line?"

I nodded, before realising it was a phone call! "Yes, that's fine."

"Great, thanks, Line. Just to let you know, we have just brought Kenneth Hansen into the station for questioning, for the murder of his wife, Heidi Hansen."

"Oh, wow. Is he arrested?"

"No, not yet, Line. We will be holding him for at least 12 hours, though," he replied.

"So, I'm safe to go to work then? Like, on a bus?"

"Yes, Line, you are safe to go to work however you wish," he laughed gently.

"Ok, so what happens now?"

"Well, we'll be questioning his movements. From what I can tell, he was seen close to both scenes while they were happening, so we'll be doing forensics too."

"Ok, thanks," I replied.

"We'll contact you before he's released, so that you know. If we deem him a threat to you, we'll assess what level of threat it is. If it is a high level, then we'll keep him in, otherwise we can issue him with a restraining order to keep away from you, seeing as he approached you yesterday."

"Ok," I smiled, brightening up a bit.

"Have a great day," he replied, ending the call.

I laid back down for a second, to process the information received. The sun was peeping through my curtains, so decided to get up! 'I can work, after all', I thought.

I jumped in the shower, singing as I scrubbed, then dressed and went to the kitchen for sustenance. Thoughts of coffee made my stomach turn, despite loving the smell coming from the pot that was percolating. Instead, I opted for the orange juice carton that was at the back of the fridge, and poured a glass of that.

I checked through my phone and found several text messages. Pappa had messaged me to check if it was this weekend that I'd be cleaning the flat and changing the locks. Erik had sent a couple of messages, checking if I was ok. I returned his message straight away.

'I'm ok. Sorry for not replying sooner, it's been a very strange few days. Speak soon?'.

I started replying to Pappa's text when I received a call from Erik.

"Hey, Miss U. Are you ok?" he began.

"Yes, thanks," I replied.

"So what's been going on then?"

I gave him a rough breakdown of all that had happened.

"Oh my God, Line, why didn't you contact me sooner?"

"I'm sorry, it's just been… like everything is a blur and fuzzy. It's difficult to explain."

"Want to catch up later?" he asked.

"Most definitely!" I replied enthusiastically.

"Shall I meet you after work?" he suggested.

I hadn't confirmed that I was going in today. Should I check with Marit first?

"Line?"

"Sorry, yes, well… at Olsen's at around 14:30?" I figured that I could change this if Marit didn't want me to work, or needed me to work late to make up for arriving late.

"See you later, then."

I poured myself another glass of orange, smaller this time, and I managed a slice of toast too, before heading out for a bus to work.

Marit protested when I first arrived, but I explained that I needed to work to keep my mind occupied. I set to it straight away, seeing as I'd missed the first couple of hours or so.

The day went very quickly, and Erik arrived at the office building as arranged.

"Hi," he said, smiling, "Miss U!"

I beamed at him; I hadn't realised how much I had missed him. We ended up back at Marit's, drinking and chatting.

"Aren't you sick of this place?" Marit laughed, as she brought our food and drink to us.

"Nope, this is one of my favourite places," I smiled at her.

I had offered to work until the café closed, but she emphatically said no, as she'd told me to take at least two days off work. The least I could do was spend my 'café' money there.

I explained all that had happened in more detail to Erik.

"So he's at the station now, then?" he asked.

I pulled my phone out my bag to check for messages. "As far as I'm aware," I replied, "the guy said he'd let me know when he's released."

"Cool. What do you fancy doing then?"

"I'm pretty tired really…" I replied.

"Oh, ok," he replied glumly.

"Oh, no I wasn't trying to get rid of you! I meant that we could go back to my new home?"

"Sure thing!"

"Are you working tonight?" I asked.

"Nope!" he replied.

"Excellent!"

We said goodbye to Marit and left the coffee shop. A flash of lightning lit up the whole sky.

"Now that's lightning!" Erik joked.

I laughed, then paused for a moment. "Actually, can we take a little detour?"

Erik nodded and smiled.

We crossed the road and walked in the opposite direction to my apartment until we arrived at a rundown-looking, brown-bricked, tall building.

"Is this your new place?" Erik questioned.

"No, my place is much nicer," I smiled, pressing all of the intercom buzzers.

The main door unlocked, and I dragged him inside. "We're looking for number 34," I told him.

As we approached the door of number 34, Erik asked me whose home it was.

"Hansen's," I whispered.

"Holy cow, Line!"

"I'll only be a couple of minutes – a quick 'in and out'. Can you keep a look out please?"

Before he could reply, I swiped my bank card in the lock to unlock it and slipped inside. The place was an utter mess, much worse than Thor and Kristian had managed, although I'd find out for sure at the weekend! I stepped over piles of rubbish and newspapers, making sure that I didn't disturb anything, although I doubted that he'd notice!

I had no intention of going into his bedroom or bathroom, so headed towards the kitchen. Just at the doorway, there was an old desk. It was strewn with ash from his cigarettes, an ashtray filled to the brim, and a brown envelope. I pulled a tissue out of my trouser pocket and moved the envelope slightly, memorising where it had been. As I did this, I noticed a pile of white papers. I turned one over and it was a photograph of me and Erik at the aquarium. I gasped. He had followed us all the way there? I picked up another, and another, and another, and they were all of me; at Frogner Park the other week; outside Olsen's when I was with Heidi, moments before she was murdered; me in my new apartment.

I couldn't breathe. I felt like something, or someone was holding something over my mouth. I looked inside the brown envelope and there were endless photos of me with Erik. The envelope was addressed to Thor at the old flat. I took photos of everything on that desk, and placed everything back where it was.

My mobile phone rang in my bag. I rummaged to answer it.

"Yes?" I answered breathlessly.

"Hi, Line, its Stefan Jakobsen, from Oslo Police. Just letting you know that we have had to let Mr Hansen go. There wasn't enough evidence to arrest him. If you want to come in, then you can fill out some paperwork to get the restraining order?"

I laughed at the irony. "I'm not feeling too good right now, can I arrange it another time?"

"Sure thing, Line, you have my number if you need me?"

"Yes, thanks… Mr… Mr…"

I ended the call, tiptoed round the rubbish and exited the flat.

"This is so wrong," Erik said, looking nervous.

"I'm so sorry, Erik, it was wrong of me. Let's go?"

He nodded and led me out of the building. I let go of his hand and ran behind the building to throw up.

"Oh my God, are you ok, Line?"

"I'm so sorry," I apologised again, wiping my mouth.

He passed me his bottle of water. The rain came faster and he held me close to keep me as dry as possible.

"I went one step too far!" I continued. "He's been released, we need to get out of here!"

We crossed the road and jumped on the next bus.

Back at my apartment, I shakily made us both drinks and sat on my sofa. I passed him a towel for his hair after the rainstorm.

"I'm so sorry, Erik," I repeated. "I was clearly out of my depth, and I dragged you into it!"

Erik shook his head. "What did you find?" he enquired.

"As expected – photos, LOTS of photos! Of me, of US! TOGETHER!!"

I drank some milk to settle my stomach, and showed him the pictures on my phone.

"There were loads in an envelope addressed to… to…"

"Your ex?"

"Yes!"

I felt awkward even mentioning Thor to Erik. The shame would probably be with me forever.

"I feel so shit," I sighed, "I'm clearly a rubbish investigator!" I laughed, closing my eyes.

Chapter 29 – Door Ajar

I awoke very early the next morning. I was still on the sofa, where I had, or thought I had, closed my eyes for just a second. I sat bolt upright, wondering where Erik was, but I couldn't locate him in the dark. My phone was still next to me, so I clicked it and found that it was 03:35.

I stood up and wandered around to see if I could see Erik, but there was no sign. I clicked the kettle on and grabbed a mug, then changed my mind and just filled it up with milk instead. I had a quick shower and got dressed. I checked the time again and it was only 04:00, so I decided to head for the gym. I packed a small bag with clothes to change into and a towel, plugged my earphones in and made my way to the bus stop.

I avoided the lounge as I didn't want to waste any time, and changed into my kit. I found myself struggling with the equipment, it had clearly been too long since I had been there. I chose the exercise bike, instead, for some gentle cycling at a slower pace.

When it was time to leave, I showered, changed and returned to the main reception. I saw on the notice board that there was a yoga session that afternoon at 5 p.m., so made a mental note to attend this.

The bus dropped me off just a couple of buildings away from the café, but I still unplugged my earphones to remain aware of my surroundings. I figured it could be too early for Hansen, as he had always been 'on time' for work, at 8 a.m. usually. No need to lower my defences though!

Marit arrived at around the same time that I did, and scolded me for being on my own when she opened the door for me.

"It's ok, I've kept an eye out," I soothed her, heading to the staff area.

"Coffee?" she offered.

I shook my head. "Would it be too expensive to have milk? I can pay the extra?"

"Don't be silly, of course you can have milk. Gone off coffee?"

"I'm not sure. I think I may be associating coffee with working with Hansen, and from living with Thor and Kristian."

"Fair enough, as long as it's not my coffee!"

I shook my head again. "People would pay millions for your coffee!" I thought for a few seconds. "Hey, have you ever considered selling packs of the coffee beans that you use? Or would it mean less customers as a result?"

"Hmmm..." Marit mused, "I'm not sure. I'll have a think."

I smiled and set about cleaning the customer areas.

"Are you doing anything nice tonight?" Marit chatted to me as we worked.

"My gym has a yoga class at five o'clock, so thought I might try it out. You?"

"Ooh that sounds good. My boyfriend has a late meeting at work, so it looks like a quiet night in for me!"

I realised that I knew nothing about my boss.

"My gym allows members to bring a friend to a class or gym session. Did you want to come?" I suggested.

"I may just take up that offer!"

"I usually stay at Olsen's till he closes, so I can always pop back when you're ready to close up?"

Marit nodded and smiled. She opened up the doors and returned to the counters. The first customer in was Erik. He beamed at me and I smiled back.

"If I'd known you were waiting, I'd have let you in!" Marit appeared from behind me.

He sat down at one of the tables and Marit nodded in approval, allowing me to sit with him for a few minutes, until it got busy. He pulled his phone out and downloaded the app.

"You don't need the app, I owe you more than enough." I paused to think. "I forgot to ask how much I need to give you for that meal?"

He shook his head. "It doesn't matter," he replied.

"No, no not a chance, mister, I will be paying you back! I'm so sorry that I fell asleep last night."

"I'll try not to take it personally," he laughed. "I left you to sleep a bit, then slipped out and went home. I did contemplate waking you up so you could go to bed, but you looked really comfortable…"

"Thank you," I smiled. "Are you working today?"

"Yeah. Start at 11 a.m. and finish as 11 p.m.," he explained.

"Wow! That's a long day."

He ordered a coffee and a sandwich on the app. "What do you think to the app?" I enquired.

"It's great – nice and simple."

I smiled, "Thanks for all of your help."

"Glad to help."

"Oh, I just remembered… thinking back to that day at the aquarium, when you gave me your brilliant advice, I found some photos of us in **Drøbak in Hansen's flat**!"

"Jesus! So he followed us?" he exclaimed, visibly shocked.

"He must have," I shrugged, standing up as more customers arrived.

Erik's table was right next to the till, so I could still stand and chat to him when I wasn't cleaning or serving. He watched me as I worked, smiling at me. I watched him and smiled as he ate. His vibrant blue eyes flashed when the light caught them. His blonde curls bounced as he moved. He was a delight to look at.

He tapped on his phone screen a couple of times, then looked up at me. "I'm off now, plus you need the table for other customers. I'll call you tomorrow?"

I nodded enthusiastically, and watched as he walked out.

"He sure is scrumptious, isn't he?!" Marit said, also admiring him leaving.

"Hey, stop looking, he's mine!" I replied.

"Is he now?!" Marit raised her eyebrows at me.

I giggled, then became more serious. "I just feel so guilty for hurting him when I hooked up with Thor…"

"He seems ok with you now though, doesn't he?"

I nodded, as I filled my glass up with milk behind the counter. "He seems to have boundaries, he's not tried to make a move."

"Give it time," Marit advised.

I found that there was a new notification on the till's app screen, and discovered that Erik had left a five star review for the café. I showed Marit. She beamed.

"Fantastic!" she exclaimed.

I looked at the available sandwiches. "The cream cheese has garlic in, doesn't it?" I enquired.

Marit nodded. I chose tuna and mayonnaise instead, as I didn't fancy garlic. I took my lunch and a coffee over to Olsen's, as Einar came to collect me, to escort me.

"I managed to get buses to the gym and work this morning," I informed him.

"It's not going to stop me from being protective towards you," he replied, smiling and opening the office's door for me.

"I appreciate it, thank you, Einar."

I sat in my usual spot behind the desk and munched on my sandwich. 'It's nice to have a change', I thought to myself. Einar decided that it looked delicious too and ordered it for his lunch later. He escorted me back to work, and I thanked him. He ordered a fruit slushie from the takeaway section. It was exceptionally hot, and this was reflected in the queues for slushies. 'We could do with, maybe two takeaway sections', I mused. 'One for general food and one for cold drinks, maybe?'.

The afternoon was fast-paced with a flurry of customers, too many for all of the seating that we had. I apologised, and pulled out and cleaned two of the chairs from the staff area and placed them behind the chairs of the takeaway section, with just the roller banner between them, for an elderly couple to sit and wait. I asked if they wanted a drink while they waited, and the gentleman came to the counter to order. He mopped his brow with a handkerchief.

"It is very warm today, isn't it?" I commented, striking up a conversation with him.

"Too warm!" he replied. "I live in Norway for the cold weather!"

"It'll soon be cold and dark! Then we'll all be moaning about that!"

"I'd rather have a cold, dark day any time."

"Would you prefer a fruit slushie instead of a hot drink?" I suggested.

"I'm rather stuck in my ways, dearie, but thank you."

As soon as a table became available, I quickly cleaned it and escorted them over, with Marit bringing over their drinks at the same time.

"That was excellent, Line. You are doing so well, and coming up with some great ideas. I'll order a couple more chairs to replace those. Really brilliant!"

I showed the couple how to download the café's app for them to try, and they were pleased with how easy it was.

I showed them how to leave a review too, "…just in case you are happy with our café, of course!"

Marit had similar ideas in mind and had quickly designed and printed off some circular, bold stickers to be added to the menu near the app info section. We did a little high five under the counter.

It was soon time for me to go, so I took Einar's lunch and headed for the office building. I was surprised that he hadn't appeared to escort me again; I figured he was busy. As I walked closer to his business, I noticed that the door was open. I had a sharp intake of breath as panic washed over me.

"Hello, Mr Olsen?" I called, using his official name, in case his tenants were around.

There was no answer. I wasn't sure if I should go inside or stay outside. I peered through the gap in the door and saw a woman laying on the floor in the reception area. It looked like Einar was standing over her. Another wave of panic swept over me as I realised that it could have been Einar that murdered... No, that couldn't be.

"Hello..?" I called out again.

Einar swung his head around to look at me. I was so nervous that I could feel my legs shaking. My fight or flight mode was usually to fly, but my legs wouldn't move.

"Ah, Line, come in!" he beckoned me. "This poor lady has just fainted. It must be the heat," he explained.

"Have you...ha.. have you called for an ambulance?"

"No, my phone is behind the desk. Can you call for me please?"

I remained in the doorway, and grappled in my bag for my phone. My hands were shaking as I dialled.

"Hello. Where's your emergency?" the operator asked.

"Olsen Business Services, in Kirkegata," I replied.

"What's going on there?"

"There's a lady who has collapsed in the reception area. I think she's fainted."

"What's your name?"

"Line Larsen."

"Ok, Line, is she breathing?"

"I'm not with her," I explained breathlessly. "I ... can't ... It's my anxiety, I think I'm having a panic attack!"

"Ok, I'm going to need you to keep calm for me, Line. Is anyone with her?"

"Y..yes, the business owner, Mr Olsen." I wanted to make sure they knew he was in there.

"Can you ask him if she's breathing?"

"Is she breathing, Mr Olsen?"

"Yes, she is. She's conscious now, but very groggy. I think she's pregnant."

"Hello," I spoke back to the operator, "he said..."

"I heard him, thank you, Line," she confirmed. "We have despatched someone to your address now. How are you doing?"

"I ... I.. witnessed a murder here a few weeks ago, well, I got there after the murder. In the…the same… building… I just…can't…"

"Keep breathing, Line, someone will be there very soon."

"Thank…"

The call disconnected and I slid to the floor, trying to control my breathing. I closed my eyes until the paramedics arrived. One of them went through the doors to the reception, and the other crouched down to talk to me.

"Hi, are you Line?" he asked.

I nodded, sweating profusely.

"Shall we get you indoors?" he suggested.

"Murder… there was a murder…"

"When, Line?" the paramedic exclaimed.

"A few weeks ago… I found her… I can't go in there…"

"Ah, ok, Line. I seem to remember you from then as I was working that day too." He looked around the door. "The lady seems fine, she's sitting on a chair and drinking some water. She's fine."

Einar arrived at the door. "Oh, Line, it must have been so scary for you, after Mrs Johnsen. Come on, it's safe now, she only fainted."

The paramedic helped me up and walked me toward the building door.

I stopped just past the door, and turned to the paramedic. "Do you need me to be here?" I enquired.

He shook his head. "I think you should sit down for a minute."

"Can I go back to work please? Here's the order for Mr Olsen, if you could pass it on? I just... can't go in there right now."

"Ok, Line, where is your work?" I pointed to Marit's. "The coffee shop?" I nodded.

"Ok do you want me to go in with you?" he offered.

I laughed. "It's funny, I've only worked there a few weeks, but I've brought her nothing but drama!"

"Ok," he laughed too, "if I need anything else from you, I'll pop in?"

I nodded and he let me go. I walked through the door and straight through to the staff area. Marit followed me in.

"Are you ok, Line?" she enquired.

"I'm sorry," I replied. "Can I just stay here a short while please?"

"Sure, do you need anything?" she asked.

"You go back to work," I said, shaking my head, "I'm enough of a pain as it is," I tried to laugh.

I felt very faint and as soon as she left, I slid from the chair to sit on the floor. The tiles were cool to the touch, which was perfect. I laid down for a couple of minutes, just appreciating the coldness. I laid still until I felt well enough to sit back on the chair. I was just getting up to the chair when Einar appeared.

"Oh, goodness, are you ok, Line? Do you want me to fetch the paramedic back?" he offered.

I shook my head. "I'm fine, thanks, Einar. It just brought back memories of..."

"I'm so sorry, Line. It was just unfortunate timing. Let me take you back to the off…"

"No, No… I'd rather stay here, if you don't mind?"

"Of course not," he spoke quietly. "I'll see you soon?"

I nodded and tried to smile. He held the chair for me so I could be seated again, and then left. I burst into tears.

I remained alone until the tears subsided. I was disappointed that I was feeling so weak and vulnerable, but realised that I'd put so much trust in someone who could potentially be the actual killer. Maybe Hansen was telling the truth? It could have been Einar all along? 'He has a spare key to the apartment,' I thought, 'I need to get a spare lock, just in case'.

I pulled myself together, washed my face in the bathroom sink and grabbed my bag. I re-entered the shop, and saw the clock was showing at around 15:30, giving me ample time to go to the shops in the city.

"I'll see you back here at 5 p.m.?" I checked with Marit as I left.

"Be safe," she replied.

I plugged my headphones in and started my quest.

In a large homeware store, I found a chain lock and a screwdriver. I put it into a basket and browsed. 'Retail therapy works wonders', I thought. I loved my new home and I wasn't going to allow my landlord being a potential murderer put me off. I laughed to myself. 'I'm pretty sure that I'm going to get murdered, one way or another', I thought.

I grabbed some cheerful yellow crockery and cutlery, and a bamboo fruit bowl and matching utensil holder. I even found a hook to hang bananas on. I paid for everything and then ventured to a food store. My cupboards were fairly well-stocked, but I really wanted to get some fruit in, along with more milk. I chose long-life milk, as I knew the shopping would be hanging around in my gym locker for a few hours.

Yes, I still intended to go to the yoga session! Just because I was going to be murdered, there was no need to stop living until then! I bought a bag of ice and found an insulated bag for frozen food at the checkout. On my way back to Marit's, I spotted a shop that sold kitchen utensils, and realised that I didn't actually have any to put in my new pot. I laughed to myself and went inside. Amongst the array of utensils, I discovered pots and pans, and even stickers for my kitchen tiles. I chose the sunflower design, and picked up some yellow saucepans and a frying pan. 'It's a good job that I have a large locker at the gym!', I thought as I lifted the heavy bag of kitchen delights from the counter, behind which a bored-looking assistant was checking her watch. She followed me out and changed the sign to '**Closed**', switching off the lights and locking the door behind her.

I headed back to the coffee shop to wait for Marit to finish up her work, and then we both walked to the gym. We chatted excitedly during the journey, like little schoolchildren on a trip. Marit had never tried yoga before, so it was a little daunting for her, but she seemed confident that I'd be there for her. We arrived with just a few minutes to spare. I had l left a bag of gym clothes at the café the other day, and as we were both roughly the same size, I lent Marit some. I popped my shopping into a bigger locker than usual, as there wasn't enough room in the one I had been using. We managed to squeeze Marit's stuff in there too.

The session felt amazing, and I felt totally de-stressed. Marit seemed to have enjoyed it too, although we both struggled with some of the positions; something we could work on. The gym lent Marit a towel so that she could shower, and we even managed a couple of minutes in their sauna. We showered and changed, and we moved to the members' lounge. Marit had just poured her first coffee when a personal trainer approached her to chat about membership. I took the opportunity to check my phone while she was distracted. There was a text message from Pappa and two from Erik. Pappa was checking the time I would be at the old flat on Saturday. 'Shit! I had forgotten about that!', I thought. 'Mustn't put it off'. I knew that the Valle brothers wouldn't be leaving for work till maybe 10ish, so I replied,

'Midday ok for you?'.

Erik's texts were just general 'hope you are having a good day' messages. I replied, telling him it had been an ok day, and that I'd explain more when I next saw him. In the time it took to do these tasks, Marit had been convinced to sign up with the gym.

"That's great!" I exclaimed, "now you are a member, you can go to the self-defence class for free!"

She nodded and grinned

I opted for a tea in the lounge; I needed some caffeine as I was feeling quite fatigued. I had been up for quite a while though!

"So what is your new home like then?" Marit asked. "I didn't get much time to take a look the other day.

"Well, to most people it could be seen as basic, but it's *my* place, and I love it!"

"That's all that matters, isn't it?"

I nodded. "You'll have to come round sometime," I suggested.

"Girls' night in," she smiled, raising her coffee cup for a toast.

I tapped her cup with my teacup and we both laughed.

Chapter 30 – Under the Makeup

I had retired to bed almost as soon as I got home after the gym, and woke up fairly early the next morning. I had a glass of milk, and gave all my new pots and pans a quick wash before putting them into cupboards and drawers. I found the safety chain for my front door, and wondered if it would be too early to try and install it right now. I placed it on my kitchen counter along with the screwdriver, and ventured into the bathroom to have a shower.

Feeling fresher, I had a quick try to fix the chain to the door, and found it quite easy, and quiet. There was time to have a quick cycle on the gym's exercise bikes and I headed to the bus stop. 'I'm definitely going to get myself a bike!', I decided. When I was using the exercise bikes, I closed my eyes and imagined the scenery I could see on many trails of nearby nature. I ensured that I would check the information board for the spin classes on the way out too.

Work was manic, the busiest day I had even experienced in the coffee shop, including when I was a customer. I remained in the staff area for my lunch, my excuse to Einar being that I may be needed if the crowds increase. In secret, though, I wasn't ready to spend time with him if he was the real killer, or stay in the building. He informed me that everyone was entitled to a decent break, but was impressed with my loyalty. I apologised and suggested that he collect his own lunch for today, and I said that I would order it in advance for him, so that he would be able to just grab and go. I made a mental note to suggest this as an option for takeaway customers, by using the app to pre-order.

I knew that Marit wouldn't allow me to work through any part of my lunch, but it was actually quite nice to have a change of scenery. I discovered a little sofa tucked away which was really comfortable. That was a game changer!

"Shhh," one voice said, "she must be really tired if she can fall asleep here."

"Do you think she's ok?" another one replied.

"She did have a long day yesterday, and it has been a stressful week for her."

I opened my eyes, and then realised that I had fallen asleep on that sofa.

"I'm so, so sorry," I mumbled. "I'll be back out front in a minute."

Marit smiled, sitting next to me. "It's ok, Line, I did say you could have a few days off, which you refused!" she fake-grimaced at me. She reached over the side of the arm of the sofa and produced a pillow and blanket. "Here, this will make it more comfortable, just take a break!"

"No, it's ok, I'll…"

"NO, you will do as you are told," she laughed gently. "Sleep, or at least rest."

~

"Line, I'm sorry to wake you, but I'm closing the shop now. I'm not allowed to have sleeping residents on the property once I'm closed!" she smiled at me.

"Shit! What time is it?" I responded.

"It's 4:45."

"Oh, I'm so sorry! I've got self-defence class."

"I've got the car just outside, so we can get there on time. Just give yourself a few minutes to wake up, while I finish up out front!"

I felt really groggy, probably due to the excess sleep, but I managed to swing my legs around and off the sofa. I stood up and grabbed my things, ready for the short journey. Marit appeared, and we left through the back door, with her going first. We arrived in what seemed like seconds, and we were a good 10 minutes early. We greeted the receptionist and proceeded to the changing rooms. I nipped into the toilet cubicle before changing into my gym clothes.

"Do you reckon she'll bother coming today?" one woman said just outside of the cubicle door.

"Highly doubt it," another replied.

"Too busy killing people," the first laughed.

"Two now, isn't it? First one inside her workplace, and the second just outside."

"Can't be her though, can it? Line is way too much of a scaredy cat to even say boo to a goose! Silly cow!"

"She managed to cheat on her boyfriend, for a guy who just wanted to control her. She told me that he'd been messing with her for months, but she deserved it for falling for his narcissistic charm. If she doesn't beg and plead for him to stay, he'll probably just leave her in the shit. Apparently, him, and his smelly brother, and I mean SMELLY, are just trashing her flat. She'll not get the deposit back, but I bet she'll still try and clean it!"

I recognised that voice, it was Bella!

"Cleaner, Line, cleaner!" the other one rhymed my name, for a joke!

They both laughed.

"Alright, girls?" a third voice asked; it was Astrid.

"Yeah," said Bella, "just debating whether the bunny boiler will bother to turn up today."

"Well, it's curry night tonight, so if she is coming, we'll have to pre-order the jugs of water!" Astrid cackled.

"I'll grab a litre of milk on the way!" the second woman said. it was Helene.

"Naaa, don't bother with all that, she won't come. Her boss-boyfriend won't let her out!" Bella laughed; they all laughed.

I sat on the closed toilet seat, not wanting to confront them. Yes, I really was all those things that they were saying about me.

"D'ya think she killed those women, then?" Helene asked.

"Nope!" Bella replied confidently. "Her boss, Kenneth Hansen, was arrested for it, wasn't he?"

"Questioned, apparently. One of my customers told me that the second woman, who as his wife, warned Line that he was going to kill her after he killed her," Astrid explained.

"Too many 'her's there, Astrid," Bella laughed.

"I know right!" she replied. "The wife told Line… right… that Line would be next… right… after the wife, who was actually murdered just a few minutes after this confrontation."

"Wow, that's confusing, Astrid!" Helene laughed. "She was having an affair with him, wasn't she?"

"With her boss, Kenneth Hansen, yeah. Have you seen the state of him? It's disgusting. Fucking marriage wrecker!"

"Do you think he killed his wife so he could move Line in with him? Steal her from her boss-boyfriend, to become her next boss-boyfriend?"

"Maybe they conspired together!"

Bella over-exaggerated a repulsive shiver. "Skank!"

Behind the door, I was allowing floods of silent tears to roll down my face, and I suddenly felt really sick. The sound of my throwing up and crying simultaneously alerted the trio of my attendance, although they may not have realised it was me until I flushed and emerged, heading for the sinks. All three faces dropped.

"I guess I don't need to invite you to my housewarming party, then," I said sarcastically, swilling my mouth out with water. "I'll find an alternative self-defence class to go to instead."

I walked off, towards Marit. She could see my face changing from fake-sarcasm to heartbreak. She stayed steady, to continue the deception for me.

"Line!" Bella exclaimed.

There was no way she could spin this to her favour.

"Hey, Line," Marit butted in, "guess we're having an early dinner, girl!"

I nodded, feeling sick to my core, retching a little at the thought of it. Marit helped me empty my locker and we left, still dressed in our gym kits.

Back in the car, I fell apart. "I'm so sorry, Marit. I thought they were my friends," I explained.

Marit nodded. There was no way that their conversation about me could be misinterpreted.

"Let's take you home."

She reached into the glove compartment and passed me a pack of tissues. I cried all the way home, and Marit helped me get into my apartment. I continued to cry and she just held me until the tears finally subsided a little.

"I'm so sorry!" we both said simultaneously.

"You have nothing to apologise for," I replied.

"What shitty friends," she remarked, shaking her head. "Have they always been that bitchy?"

"Not that I was aware of before?" I shrugged, hopelessly.

"Better out of it," Marit soothed. "When you lose one friend, you can potentially gain two new ones."

"Huh?"

"Well, my mamma always says stuff like that!"

"Mine is one of the most level-headed, aloof mothers ever!"

We both laughed a little, grateful for a change of atmosphere.

"Did you want to get any food?" Marit asked me.

I shook my head. "Not really, my mouth tastes like a dustbin and my stomach feels like a washing machine!"

"That'll be the stress catching up with you. See if you can have an early night, maybe?" she suggested. "You don't need to be at work tomorrow, so you can have a lie-in."

"Pity I don't have my sedatives anymore, hey?"

"I don't think you will need them tonight!"

She gave me a little squeeze and handed me my apartment keys. I followed her to the door so that I could add the chain lock to my enhanced security system. I crawled into bed and was asleep almost instantly.

Heidi Hansen

Chapter 31 – Barely Hanging On

I was rudely woken at around 22:00, according to my phone. There was lots of banging around, and people screaming, laughing and banging. My intercom buzzed but I just ignored it. There was loud cheering outside my door and smashing of glasses, and it sounded like it was on all levels of the building. My stomach tightened and I felt real fear. My heart was racing and my mind was swirling.

'I'm going to be murdered this weekend', I chanted in my mind.

I tiptoed, backwards, from my bedroom to my kitchen, to get a drink of water, and my new frying pan. It had quite a bit of weight to it, so would be suitable for anyone choosing to intrude.

'I'm going to be murdered this weekend', I chanted in my mind.

I returned to my bed, placed the glass on the windowsill, and the pan in bed next to me. I crouched on the bed against the headboard, pulled the covers up to my chin and stared intently at the bedroom door for the rest of the night. I gripped the pan, ready to strike anything unwanted, trembling with fear. My sweaty palms loosened my grip occasionally, but I wiped my hands on my sheet and reassumed the position.

'I'm going to be murdered this weekend', I chanted in my mind.

Eventually, the noise died down. I looked at my phone to find it was 04:00. There was still the occasional sound of someone laughing, and heels on the concrete floors. The last buzz of my intercom was around half an hour later. I continued to sit up in bed with my frying pan until it was time to get up.

'I'm going to be murdered this weekend', I chanted in my mind.

I didn't see the point of having a shower or wearing clean clothes, so I pulled my hair up into a rough ponytail, sprayed some body spray on me and headed out to catch the 07:37 bus into the city. It was rammed with people of all ages. Little kids running up and down the aisle. Babies crying. Young men who didn't even make as much effort as me with the body spray. My stomach retched at the mix of their body odour and some other's cheap aftershave.

I had a pit stop at Marit's, which made me regret my haggered look and undetermined aroma. She smiled when she saw me.

"You were meant to have a lie-in!" she wagged her finger at me.

"Noisy, drunk neighbours," I responded, rolling my eyes.

She frowned. "Milk?" I nodded and took a seat on my stool while I waited. The café was rammed with customers, more than had been there during the week. Marit whizzed off to prepare a few orders and I remained seated. I recognised the odd customer and smile politely, hoping they wouldn't ask me work stuff.

Marit returned with a brown envelope. "Your wages," she explained.

I thanked her and popped it straight into my bag. Worried that I may have someone watching me, my paranoia demanded that I take it to my locker instead, for safekeeping. I considered leaving a note with it, telling Marit to give it to my parents if I'm murdered, but couldn't find a pen. I made a mental note to tell Marit when she had a spare minute. I decided to remain in the staff area after discovering a hole at the knee of my jeans; I couldn't be seen representing Marit's business looking so shoddy. I sat and absentmindedly picked at my jeans' hole, making it bigger.

My mind started replaying the events of the last few weeks. Who was this killer on the loose?

Hansen had been the prime suspect for a while, and even his wife thought it was him. He had been in the building when Aggie was murdered, and was trying to lure Heidi into his car just minutes before she was stabbed.

Einar? Where was he when Aggie was killed? I thought back to the movements of that day. He had been there that day, but left around the same time as I did, I think? Could he have discreetly returned, killed her and left before I returned? He was around when Heidi was killed. Then there was that woman who had 'fainted' at the office. Had she really fainted? The paramedics seemed to think so!

It was the same paramedic who attended both times. Could he be connected somehow? Was I clutching at straws with this theory?

 Whoever it was, I knew I was the next target.

The paramedic didn't know where I lived, but he hadn't known where Aggie lived either.

Einar, on the other hand, DID know where I lived, and had keys to my apartment. He could hide inside at any time, ready to pounce. Or, he may prefer the office to kill? But it was ruining his business. That didn't make sense.

Hansen: he could easily just 'accidentally' bump into me, on a day just like today, slide a knife into me, and then just carry on walking. Oh, wait, he also knew my address, as he'd taken photos of me at my apartment! Could he kill wherever the opportunity rose?

Either way, there was no set place or time to where or when I could be murdered.

I drained my glass and cheerfully waved goodbye to Marit. I headed into the homeware store that I visited yesterday, to pick up some cleaning supplies.

"Cleaner, Line, CLEANER!" The words from my friend's mouth reverberated through my head.

I mentally shook them out of my mind.

I took a different route to the flat, to avoid the brothers' usual path to work. I hesitated for a moment when I heard Kristian's voice nearby. Great! They had left for work! I heard Thor reprimand his brother for something. No change there – I certainly didn't miss either of them! I peered around the wall and saw them walking away. I also noticed a car, which looked identical to Hansen's, crawl around the corner as the boys crossed the road.

I waited until it passed, then crossed the road towards the flat. I jogged up the stairs and fumbled with my keys to unlock the door quietly. I wasn't sure if they would have any 'houseguests'. I tiptoed around but there was no one loitering. There were no curtains up to replace the ones I took with me. The place was worse than I expected, especially as it had only been a week. There were actual puddles of what I assumed to be beer, soaking into the carpet. There was pizza stuck to the ceiling – THE CEILING!

In the kitchen, there were the remnants of what looked like a hot oil fire. Burnt cloths were in the sink, and the floor. I moved one with my foot and discovered a scorched circle, around the size of the bottom of the saucepan on the vinyl floor. I didn't want to investigate the rest of the flat; not yet.

I took a moment to just cry.

I pulled the bin bags that I'd just purchased out of the bag, and separated the first one, tearing through the bottom. I cursed, and tried again with the next one. At that moment, I heard a noise outside the door. It was Kristian. I dashed behind the breakfast bar to hide, but he spotted me.

"What the hell are you doing here?!" he boomed.

"My name's on the tenancy agreement, not yours!" I retorted bravely.

"You abandoned it."

"I told you that you only had a week or so to get this place clean."

"We ain't going nowhere!"

"Yes, you are!" I replied, slowly realising that I had no way to reinforce this.

He walked towards me. "You and whose army?"

I opened my mouth and shut it again. He pressed against me, face to face. He reached behind me, and I heard the sound of metal scraping. He brought a knife up and held the cold metal against my face.

I held my breath.

"Your friends tried to chat shit about me, but I shown them who's boss!"

"My friends?"

"Woman at the office. Mad wife of your boss. I learnt them a lesson!"

His eyes widened maniacally, and he pressed the knife's edge into my face.

"You?" I exclaimed between breaths., my legs shaking uncontrollably.

"In between the first and second ribs – don't even feel it at first. Learnt that from TV, even though you reckoned it were all trash," he explained, turning to look at the TV. I took the opportunity to push him away from me, and made a dash for the front door.

I didn't get far before he grabbed me. I swung round and kicked the knife out of his hand, just as they had taught us in self-defence class, when I 'bothered to attend'! It slid across the breakfast bar and onto the kitchen floor. He punched me square on my nose and I heard it crunch. I made another run for it and he rugby-tackled me, pulling my feet from under me. I couldn't breathe. He dragged me across the floor by my leg, and it seemed like his intention was to get the knife, or another one.

I kicked him until I could break free. I ran towards the door again, managing to open it before being thrown across the living area. I ran again and he pushed me to the floor. I squirmed in his hands, until I ended up laying on my front. He pulled me over by my hand, and I pain seared up my arm. He then held me down with one hand and started to undo my jeans.

"NO!" I screeched several times, scratching his neck with my nails. "HELP!" I yelled, hoping to get someone's attention.

He was now holding me by my thighs. I tried to kick him but his weight was on my feet. He pulled my jeans further down and kissed me. I bit his lip until I could taste blood. He screamed and grabbed his pillow from the sofa, pushing it against my face. The smell of it made me retch, but I couldn't breathe. He held it firmly, presumably with his head as I could hear his heavy breathing, while fumbling with my underwear.

I tried to scream, but couldn't get my breath.

I wriggled the best I could, but he was too strong.

I couldn't breathe.

'I'm NOT going to be murdered this weekend', I chanted in my mind.

I felt him push my legs apart, and I tried to free myself again.

He lifted his head again, as he no longer needed his hands to manoeuvre himself below; instead his hands held down the pillow.

I couldn't breathe.

'I'm NOT going to be murdered this weekend', I chanted in my mind.

"Do you reckon she'll bother coming today?" Bella's voice ran through my mind. *"Too busy killing people."*

"Can't be her though, can it? Line is way too much of a scaredy cat to even say boo to a goose! Silly cow!"

My best friend.

"Scaredy cat!"

Was that how I was viewed? Was I that bad a friend?

"Silly cow!"

I guess I was!

"She managed to cheat on her boyfriend, for a guy who just wanted to control her."

I'd regretted that for so long. I didn't deserve to have Erik as a friend. Maybe I deserved all I was getting, right now! Karma's a bitch.

I couldn't breathe.

I stopped resisting and fighting, letting my body go limp.

"...she deserved it for falling for his narcissistic charm... Apparently, him, and his smelly brother, and I mean SMELLY, are just trashing her flat. She'll not get the deposit back, but I bet she'll still try and clean it!"

"Cleaner, Line, cleaner!"

'I AM going to be murdered this weekend', I chanted in my mind.

32 – Solace

"From what I heard, Mr Larsen, your daughter managed to kick away the knife that had been used to kill the other two women, and she fought hard! *Really* hard. She sustained some terrible injuries during the attack. I'm sure the officer…erm…Jakobsen… will tell you more about this case. The assailant, Valle…? he could have easily become a serial killer if your daughter hadn't got the knife away and called for help. I think Jakobsen is due in soon, he's just sorting out the questioning of the murderer."

"So it was definitely him that had murdered the other two women then? Was there a connection between them all?"

"I'm not 100% sure, Mr Larsen. I'm sure Jakobsen can answer all of those questions. What I *can* tell you, is what her injuries were. He tried to stab her, but as you know she kicked the knife away. He must have been quite close to her, as the knife managed to cause a very large gash in the left side of her chest, just below her breast. She lost quite a bit of blood."

"There are head injuries, as you can plainly see, looks like blunt force trauma; would have been a heavy object. There are defensive wounds on her arms and legs, from when he…he removed the bottom half of her clothes, when he… are you sure you want all of these details, Mr Larsen?"

"Yes, please, Doctor."

"Is it ok if I leave for this part, Pappa Filip?"

"Oh, sorry, Catrine, of course you can. Go and get a bit of fresh air, you look a bit pale."

"Thanks, Pappa."

"Thanks, Doctor, please continue."

"Ok, as he pulled down the bottom half of her clothes, he would have scratches on him too, as she had skin cells under her nails. A clever girl, that daughter of yours. He raped her, there was semen inside her. The forensic team can give more information than I can, for sure."

"Oh, Filip, how is our daughter?"

"Hello, Erle. Doctor, this is my wife, Line's mother, and our daughter, Lillianne."

"Mrs Larsen. Miss Larsen."

"What happened to her, Pappa?"

"Oh, I don't quite know what to tell you."

"Mr Larsen, I'm going to leave you to it for now. I will be back a bit later, or you can page me if you need me sooner."

"Pappa?"

"I don't know how much you want to know, Lilli."

"Look, Catrine is downstairs somewhere. She was looking a little green around the gills. Go find her and let me talk to Mamma, then we can know how to proceed."

"I don't want to leave her, Pappa?"

"Just give us a few minutes, Lillianne."

"Ok, Mamma."

"Oh, Line, what happened to you, my sweetheart? Filip?"

"The Valle boy, Kristian. Apparently he was the one who killed Line's friend, along with that other woman that was murdered the other day, that had just been warning Line that they both were in danger."

"Kristian? I can't believe it. Line is far more intelligent than him; far more!"

"It wasn't intelligence, Erle, it was strength. Line had been going to self-defence classes and managed to kick the knife away from him."

"So why is she lying here then?"

"I don't know the full details but..."

"Just tell me, Filip!"

"She was beaten, badly, raped and smothered with a pillow."

"Oh, not my baby?"

"She fought hard, Erle."

"Oh, Filip!"

"How do we possibly tell her sister all this?"

"She's strong, she's a Larsen! She can take it! Larsen girls are strong!"

"Are they though, Erle? Would she be lying here if she was strong?"

"It could have been so much worse."

"Mr and Mrs Larsen?"

"Yes, dear?"

"Hi, I'm Marit, a friend of Line's. I just heard… I only saw her about an hour before all this!"

"What have you heard, Marit?"

"That the murderer got to her?!"

"Shhh… Marit, here's a tissue for you."

"I…I…If I'd known, I would have made her stay at my shop instead, Mr Larsen!"

"Marit, dear, it was just luck, well not luck as that is just ridiculous, more, unfortunate timing, that they ended up in the same place at the same time."

"Oh, Mrs Larsen. Was it Hansen? I m…mean Mr Hansen?"

"Mr Hansen? Oh, no, it was Kristian Valle."

"Thor's brother?"

"Yes. We're waiting for the police to come and give us more information, Marit, then hopefully we'll know more."

"It should be Line telling us."

"I know, Marit."

"Was it him who killed Aggie and Heidi then?"

"They think so, yes."

"She was such a ray of sunshine through all of the crap she was dealing with, bless her. I noticed a change in her last night, when she became very paranoid, probably because of Heidi saying that Hansen would kill her next. Then her friends…"

"Her friends, Marit?"

"We went to the gym together yesterday evening, ironically to attend a self-defence class, and her friends were talking crap about her, not realising she was just in the toilet cubicle that they were standing outside."

"WHO??!"

"I don't know their names, but she was visibly mortified by it. She didn't sleep last night, as far as I'm aware. She really thought she was going to … to…die this weekend. Then today it seemed like she had accepted that fate."

"I'm sorry to bother you, but there's only two people allowed in here at one time."

"Sorry, nurse, we'll go and find the other girls."

"Thank you, Mr Larsen, Mrs Larsen."

"Oh, Line. What happened? We were so sure it was Hansen. Why did he do this?"

"Hi."

"Oh, hi. I'm Marit, Line's boss."

"Hi Marit, I'm Lillianne, her sister."

"Ahh, Lilli, I've heard so much about you."

"Do you have any idea why this happened, Marit?"

"None. We thought it was her ex-boss, Mr Hansen. Then the last couple of days she thought it was the guy who owns Olsen's, and as she started living at one of his apartments, it really brought her down. They'd become good friends, she used to eat lunch with him every day until the other day when someone collapsed in the reception area and it brought back all the memories of what happened with Aggie, and she thought it was him who had murdered her."

"And all this time, she had been living with that psycho!"

"She really hated him. She fell out of love with Thor quite a while ago, and Kristian being there too just broke her."

"Marit!"
"Oh, Erik!"

"I just heard! I messaged her, to check it wasn't her, but when the reporter said that the victim had lived with that…that cretin, I just knew it was her. I should have protected her more!"

"Hi Erik, I'm Lilli, Line's sister. This is Catrine. Don't beat yourself up about it, Erik, she's always spoke so highly of you."

"I love her, Lilli, I always have."

"I know."

"Why didn't any of us work out it was him; them?"

"No idea, even Line didn't know though?"

"It must have been awful for her…"

"Shhhh…"

"Sorry, I know you guys are her family and probably don't want to hear it."

"Mamma and Pappa know all the details, but they are deciding how much to tell us, I think."

"Wow. There's a lot of people here!"

"Hi, Pappa, this is Erik, Line's... friend? Ex? Boyfriend?"

"I don't know."

"Mamma is on her way up. The policeman is on his way. I think we're only allowed two people here, but I'm sure we can speak to the police in another room."

"No, not at all. I can take Erik down to the cafeteria, although I doubt it'll be anywhere near decent!"

"Catrine and I can join you, for now?"

"That's great, girls, Erik. We'll come to you as soon as we can."

~

"Mr and Mrs Larsen, I'm Overkonstabel Stefan Jakobsen. This is Konstabel Nils Arud."

"Hello. What can you tell us?"

"Of course, Mrs Larsen. So, we were called to the flat by the landlord, who lives below Line's flat. He said that he'd heard someone shouting for help and lots of thudding and screaming."

"Yes, he contacted me too, as we know each other. That's how Line got the flat."

"Ah, good, sorry we didn't get to contacting you before him. It must have been a shock, Mrs Larsen?"

"Very much so."

"Well, the scene was terrible. The men that had lived there after Line moved out had trashed the place."

"She only moved out a week ago."

"Yes, I think she told me. I'll make a note of that. Konstabel?"

"When we arrived at the property, the suspect had attempted to leave the scene when he heard the sirens. He was wielding a knife and waving it around. He attempted to slash his wrists, but we managed to overwhelm him. He was disabled and handcuffed.

"The victim was unconscious when we got to the property. She had a pillow by the side of her, and it appeared that he had used it to suffocate her. There was a broken table in close proximity, and it looks like he used this to strike her..."

"No, he threw me against it! From the front door."

The four other people in the room swung around to look at me.

"Oh, Line, You're awake! I'll get the doctor."

"Can I have a drink please?" I asked hoarsely.

I couldn't move an awful lot and my mouth was incredibly dry, and tasted metallic.

Pappa looked at the doctor to check, who nodded approvingly.

Pappa poured some water into a cup and put a straw in it. "Just small sips."

I tried to sit up. "Don't try to move just yet, Miss Larsen, you have several broken ribs and a collarbone injury," the doctor explained.

He checked my vitals, and arranged for a nurse to help me sit up. The pain soared through me like hot knives as she raised the top half of the bed.

"Ahhh!" I cried out.

"Sorry, Line, I'll arrange to get you some more pain meds."

She disappeared out of the door and around the corner.

"Do you remember me, Line?" The overkonstabel questioned. I nodded. "Good. I'm going to need to ask you some questions, fairly soon."

I tried to reach for my water, but Pappa stopped me. As I pulled my arm back, I noticed the bruises on my wrist. A flash of Kristian holding me down by the wrist while he tore off my jeans blinded me. I gasped.

"The nurse will be here with pain medication," Mamma re-told me, as she examined every existing pharmaceutical in my vicinity. "You're not giving her that!" she instructed the nurse.

"I'm going to leave you to your family and friends for a short time, but do need your statement very soon. We'll give you an hour," the overkonstabel announced.

I nodded.

"Ok," the doctor said, "try to limit visitors to two at a time, especially with Line being so weak still. She needs some quiet recovery time."

"Thank you, Doctor," my pappa said. "I shall alert the hordes!" he joked.

I closed my eyes briefly, to try and shut out the visions from my memory. I was alive, yes, but had terrible scarring on the horizon, internally and externally.

"Line!" a shrill voice announced.

I opened my eyes and saw a mass of balloons.

"Balloons, already? How long have I been here?" I laughed, wincing with the pain.

"Gift shop," Marit smiled.

"We're so happy you are ok," Catrine announced.

"Catrine, hi?"

"Hi," she leaned over to hug me; I winced again. "Sorry," she whispered.

The balloons parted, like something out of a movie, and Erik appeared. I smiled, and felt my face tighten.

"Be careful, Miss U. You have some little war wounds!" He leant over to kiss me gently on the forehead.

"I love you too," I whispered in his ear.

"Now, now, I can see four people in here!" the doctor reprimanded.

"Sorry, kids. Can I just have a couple of minutes alone with Line?" They all stood up and shuffled outside. "Just for a few minutes," he nodded.

"Can Erik stay?" I asked, clinging onto him.

The doctor shook his head. "There are some very personal things I need to talk to you about."

I watched as they all left the room, leaving all the balloons with me.

"Ok, so Line, there are some things that I didn't want to chat to you about with others around. I hear that you lived with this man that tried to kill you, and his brother?"

"Yes, his brother was my boyfriend for a while," I confirmed.

"Ok, now, during this assault, you were raped by the assailant…" I squeezed my eyes shut tightly. "I'm sorry, Line, I know it's hard. He sexually assaulted you too?" I nodded. "Was this the first time this had happened?"

"Yes," I frowned.

"Ok, well, you were living with his brother as a couple, a sexual couple?" I nodded again. "Ok, so during the attack, it appears that you had a miscarriage. I'm terribly sorry." He looked at me with pitying eyes.

"But… I haven't slept with him, sexually, for months? I even managed to adjust my sleep pattern so that we slept and were awake at different times, simply to avoid him."

He shuffled through his papers, my charts I guess. "The embryo was about seven weeks along."

I shook my head, frowning. "There's been nobody for months…"

The doctor mirrored my frown. "And there's no chance that the… the assailant could have forced you against your will before yesterday?"

I shook my head. "I don't think Thor would have allowed it."

He looked through my charts again. "You were on sedatives following another murder?" I nodded. "These sedatives can make you have very deep sleeps. It looks like maybe the encounter, the conception, may have been during this time?" he suggested, shrugging his shoulder.

I thought hard. "Yes," I agreed.

"Ok, you can make a report and have your… ex-boyfriend arrested for this, if you want to?"

"That will mean that I have to spend more time with him; that I'll never get rid of him?"

"It's up to you, of course. Prosecuting would have it on his criminal record. A sexual assault on a young man's records can be huge. It would prevent this from happening to someone else?"

"Do I have to decide right now?"

"No, we have completed a rape check on you already, so that'll be on the younger brother's record, I'll arrange for DNA evidence for the embryo, just in case?"

"Yes, please. I'd appreciate that. But surely if he was my boyfriend and we lived together, nothing can be proven?"

"It could be worth speaking to a lawyer. Do you know any?"

'A lawyer!'. I chuckled at this.

ABOUT THE AUTHOR

Lisa is married to Rich, has 3 children, 2 granddaughters, and many cats. Born and bred in Leicester, she lived in Kent for 10 years and now resides in Derby.